Tom Wakefield was born in Cannock, Staffordshire in 1935. His father was a miner and his mother a factory worker. He wrote his first novel, *Mates*, at the age of forty. It was followed by *Drifters*, *The Discus Throwers*, *Lot's Wife* and *The Variety Artistes*. The first volume of Tom Wakefield's autobiography, *Forties' Child*, was published to great acclaim in 1980. *The Scarlet Boy*, completed by his friend, the novelist Patrick Gale, continues his account of his youth. Tom Wakefield died in 1996.

Francis King remarked that Wakefield 'had the ability to find extraordinary in the ordinary. The people he described were, by worldly standards, usually non-entities, but Wakefield would find in them something unique'.

The Scarlet Boy

Tom Wakefield

Completed by
Patrick Gale

Library of Congress Catalog Card Number: 98-84076

A catalogue record for this book is available from
the British Library on request

The right of Tom Wakefield to be identified as the author
of this work has been asserted in accordance with the
Copyright, Designs and Patents Act 1988

Copyright © The Estate of Tom Wakefield 1998

Additional material © Patrick Gale 1998

First published in 1998 by Serpent's Tail,
4 Blackstock Mews, London N4
Website: www.serpentstail.com

Set in 11pt Sabon by
Avon Dataset Limited, Bidford on Avon, Warwickshire

Printed in Great Britain by
Mackays of Chatham PLC, Chatham, Kent

10 9 8 7 6 5 4 3 2 1

CHAPTER ONE

The fireworks had not come up to Edward's expecta-
tions. For three or four weeks preceding Guy Fawkes'
Night, he had pored over the hoard. Wartime had
previously excluded this particular kind of treasure from
his childhood. The Volcano, the Jumping Jack, the
Catherine Wheel, the Super Air-Rocket, and the
iridescent Roman Candle all promised him endless
magic but the whole show had lasted just over fifteen
minutes.

'It's burning money,' his mother had muttered,
severely unimpressed by the entertainment. And Edward
had sworn not to look forward to anything ever again
with such high hopes.

When these tantalising objects had been lit, they only
provided a few seconds of action. The burnt-out cases
and shells left behind seemed to emphasise some kind
of duplicity which was connected with hope. No, only
if you expected nothing could you go pleasantly forward
and avoid disappointment. Nevertheless, whilst his
parents were out, he made his way into the front room
and looked at the garments which were laid out on the
Rexine-covered settee.

The school uniform had lain in the front room since
the beginning of September. During his lunch hour he
would rush home from his present school, pull the
curtains across the window and put on the red blazer

with the gold braid around the cuffs. As far as Edward knew, no other boy from his village had ever worn one like this before. Come next month, he could put it on.

He would travel every day, first by bus, then by train and then another bus. No-one seemed surprised that Edward had achieved a grammar school place and no-one had seemed over-enthusiastic about him taking it up. Except him.

'You'll be different from everybody else here,' his mother had said.

'I already am. I am different. I'll have to sit in the top class for three years if I stay where I am. I want to go. I've won my place,' Edward had appealed to his father.

'It's not a raffle. We'll be the losers,' his mother had observed flatly.

'Let him go. I'll pay the extras,' his father had said.

His mother had shrugged her shoulders, as if to say *you spoil him* and then given her consent.

In this year of 1950, Edward found himself attending a local secondary modern boys' school. He had been sent there prematurely on account of his primary school, a cluster of wooden huts, bulging at the seams with an overflow of children. Products of the post-war breeding spree, these were. Children of married couples making up for lost time in passion and copulation that the war had denied them. There were plans for this and plans for that; the new welfare state promised planning at all levels. Protected orgasm hadn't seemed part of the planning.

At twelve Edward found himself in the top class of the school. All the boys were larger and older than him. They bragged about their prowess in football and the size of their dicks. Edward could find little reserve of enthusiasm for football but would silently admire an erection that was displayed for show under one desk lid or another. Apart from this silent worship, it all seemed very unfair to him. He disliked the place. In this, at least, he was no different from any other of the forty-three boys in his class.

A large emphasis on woodwork, sport and gardening left Edward with a loss of self-esteem as he was good at none of these things. Boys were often caned for the smallest of misdemeanours. These legal beatings did not appear to improve discipline; they only managed to leave a sour gloom hanging about the classroom.

Edward found his days there extremely dire and sad but, thanks to infants' teachers in a previous school, he had discovered reading. He withdrew into a world of books. He absorbed one book after another, thin volumes and thick ones. Some of the other boys viewed his activity with a high degree of puzzlement and tended to regard him as though he suffered from some kind of deformity. They were sorry for him, and, for the most part, left him alone.

No accolades were delivered for reading or writing skills and Edward received little attention from his present teacher, a man who still behaved as though he were on the parade ground he had only recently left.

'So are you leaving us, boy?'

'Yes, sir.'

'When, boy?'

'End of this month. Just after half term, sir.'

The man sucked through his teeth and frowned and Edward felt like a prisoner who had revealed an escape route.

Half an hour later, Edward stood with his back to the wall in the playground. It was a stance he usually took as there was a better chance of not being knocked over. The playground was even more crowded than his classroom. At one time this had been a place of hell and

3

terror where the weak, including Edward, had been bullied by the strong. Since April, however, things had got better. Edward had acquired a protector. Edward didn't look for him now but thought about him as he gazed disinterestedly at the rough and tumble goings-on in the playing yard.

'Rural science? This bloody field has as much to do with science as my arse. It's not even gardening. Slave labour, that's what it is. You do the fork work, Edward. Leave the heavy digging to me and don't call out when we've finished. He'll only give us another patch to do.' Lawrence Brackenbury had paused in his digging and nodded toward their teacher, who stood on the outside edge of the field.

The man watched as the boys tilled the soil in readiness for planting potatoes. A great deal of effort was required but little skill. The wonder of growing things just didn't come into it. The lads were healthily occupied; an afternoon's work of this kind did no harm. The crop brought in a revenue that exceeded the rental of the field and provided the staff with a staple vegetable throughout the year. The fact that most of the boys would be put off gardening for life, didn't enter his reasoning.

In order to avoid any shirking, the boys had been paired off, one strong with one not so strong, and allocated a patch which they were forced to complete before being sent home. The field itself was part of some neglected pasture and, lying between the railway and the canal, was about three quarters of a mile away from the village.

'I'll be glad when Christmas comes and I can start work and be paid for it,' Lawrence grunted as he turned over the sods of earth.

'What are you going to do, Laurie?'

'Well, I ain't going to dig up a field that should be ploughed by horses or a tractor, that's for bloody sure. I wouldn't mind going down the pit but our mam is against it. I expect I'll work at Benmore's.'

'Benmore's?'

'Benmore's Edge and Tool Works. They make hammers and pliers and things like that.' Lawrence paused and smiled as he looked at Edward. 'I wonder what *you*'ll do, Edward? There's only women working in the library. You're too cack-handed to be in a workshop.'

'I'm not going down the pit. My dad says it won't suit me.'

'It suits him.'

'Well, I'm not him, am I?'

At a quarter to four, all the gardening tools were inspected for any traces of soil before they were stored away; silverware would have been cosseted by such scrutiny. No fork or spade was put away until its steel was soil-free and sparkling. Usually the boys wasted no time hanging about after dismissal. The delights of the surrounding countryside held little enchantment for them. They were hungry, fatigued and bored and wished to get away from the kind of punitive activity which was more reminiscent of occupation for prisoners of war than it was for students.

'Can you keep a secret, Eddie?'

'It depends on what it is.'

'There's a pair of barn owls. With fledglings. I've told nobody about them. Tell one and you tell the lot and then all the poor little buggers would be gone in no time at all. I'll show them to you if you like. You won't tell anybody?'

'No.'

'Do you want to see them?'

5

Lawrence had laid his hand casually against Edward's shoulder as he spoke and Edward looked upward, surprised to be offered such confidences by an older boy. Although he was nearly fifteen, Lawrence was tall for his age and had all the appearance of an eighteen-year-old, six foot in his stockinged feet, broad-shouldered and gangly legged. His hair, a mass of short, unruly black curls which always looked as if a high voltage of electricity had been passed through them, gave him a slightly wild, devil-may-care look. In fact, he was gentle-natured and thought and felt as most fourteen-year-olds. Edward looked twelve, but felt and thought like a sixteen-year-old.

'Yes. I've never seen barn owls. You know I won't tell anybody. Is it near?'

'Not far.' Lawrence had left his arm about Edward's shoulder in a relaxed, companionable way and Edward chose not to relinquish the proximity too quickly. Apart from the comfort it offered, there was the male scent of Lawrence, which was pleasurable to Edward's nostrils rather than nauseating.

Lawrence delighted in their surroundings and pointed out details that most other people might have missed. As they scrambled up the canal bank there was a magpie's nest in the upmost branches of a sycamore tree, which seemed to be growing on the shale. Deep in the recesses of the gorse, a tiny linnet's nest was brought into view and on the canal tow path, shoals of glittering gudgeon could be seen darting this way and that near the surface of the grey, still water.

It seemed sad to Edward that Lawrence would be moving from the school to the edge and tool works. In no time at all, his large hands would be scarred and blistered, his green eyes would be red-rimmed and bloodshot and his complexion would change from ruddy brown to grey. Before he was twenty-one, Lawrence would be classified as a grown-up.

'They're in there. You see that building this side of the canal basin?'

'It's not a barn. It can't be a barn stuck there, can it? It's derelict.'

'What's that?' Lawrence enquired. 'Dere-what?'

'Derelict. It means no longer in use. Abandoned. Left to go to rack and ruin.'

'They were stables for the barge horses. They don't use horses to pull the barges now. They are all on motors. I expect the poor old horses were all sent to the knacker's yard. But I wouldn't say the building is abandoned; some creatures are still finding shelter in it.'

The door to the stables had lost its top hinges so that both boys could squeeze through the space left at its side. Lawrence placed his forefinger first on Edward's lips and then on his own. From the inside, the place looked larger and it took Edward's eyes some time to adjust to the light. Daytime in the interior of the building was permanently dusk. Most of the woodwork about the six stalls had begun to rot and decay, there were still patches of straw strewn about the floor and the musty, damp air still exuded the strong equine smell of stables. Edward sniffed loudly.

'I can smell ghosts,' he whispered. 'I can smell phantom horses.'

'Shush, Eddie,' Lawrence quietly consoled and cajoled. 'Look. Sit here in this stall with me and talk quiet. There's nothing to be scared of.'

'Who said I was scared?' Edward settled himself next to Lawrence on the straw. 'I can still smell horses.'

'They've been gone a couple of years or more. Look. Up there in the opposite corner. Let your eyes travel along that beam, okay?'

'Yes.'

'Now. Just before the buttress intersection . . .'

'Ah,' Edward cried out. 'I see him. I see him!'

'Shush, Eddie. Shush.' Lawrence placed his hand gently over Edward's mouth. 'Don't let him know we are here. It's a her not a him, anyway. Talk quiet. Owls can get nasty when they have fledglings. Arthur Danmore had to have four stitches in his head. A pair of tawnies got at him. More fool him for trying to get at their eggs.' He glanced towards the death-like bird statuette that sat motionless on the ledge. 'I reckon she knows me. She knows I'm not going to harm her.'

'I hope you're right,' Edward observed tremulously.

Lawrence stretched out his legs and leaned back against the side of the stall. 'Just keep still. Get yourself comfortable.'

Edward took up a similar posture and the two of them sat listening for the arrival of a mate or the appearance of some young. As dusk approached, all that could be heard was the lapping water of the canal and the irritable clucking noises of a group of magpies.

Lawrence had unbuttoned his trousers.

'Look at this,' he muttered in self-admiration. He began to fumble and lovingly, slowly revealed a rigid cock. Edward was not in anyway surprised by the action. Most of the boys in his class did it. They never talked about it much but most of them did it. As far as they were concerned it was a true pleasure. He noticed that Lawrence's hand did not quite go round his cock, which was very thick. Now, aroused himself, he mirrored the activity. He saw Lawrence's legs, which had recently been bent at the knee joints, stiffen and shoot outwards. 'I wish Betty Grable would climb in through my bedroom window one night,' Lawrence

8

whispered through gritted teeth. 'Is she your favourite?'

'No. I think she's dull.'

'Who do you like then?'

'Montgomery Clift.' Edward was more involved in his personal spasms than in giving much thought to offering a more suitable answer. Lawrence paused in his activity and turned to Edward.

'Eddie, pull your trousers down and let me put my cock between your legs.'

'What? Lie on top of me?'

'It won't hurt you. I promise. Go on. Please, Eddie.'

Lawrence seemed to forget about the owls for the next five minutes or so. As he slid to and fro between Eddie's legs he thought of Betty Grable and any number of luscious beauties. For his part, when Lawrence murmured into his ear, 'Oh. I'm coming. I'm coming,' Eddie thought of Montgomery Clift but murmured nothing.

Lawrence carefully wiped away all traces of the outcome of this activity with his handkerchief.

'Alright?' he enquired gently as Edward began to pull up his trousers. Edward nodded. For some strange reason, he experienced a degree of power. He did not feel used, even if he had been a substitute for someone else. 'Look. Look!' Lawrence pointed to a gap in the broken roof. The outstretched wings hovered as the huge male bird seemed to hang in the air before it descended into the barn. Eddie watched as it left one beam and seemed to float overhead of them before it settled itself on one directly facing them. The white face and large, dark eyes gazed down at them.

Eddie, too apprehensive to move, sat up with his trousers still about his knees. Was the bird disapproving of them?

'It's alright.' Lawrence had placed an arm about Eddie's shoulder. 'He won't harm us. He knows me.'

'Have you been here before, then? I mean, with other people?'

'Only my dad. The owls have been here for years.'

'Do they have the same nest?'

'They don't build a nest. Their clutch is raised just behind those cross timbers. Sometimes they manage two clutches a year.'

'I wonder why they stay here.'

'They know where their bread is buttered. Five's is only a quarter mile away. There's plenty of mice on the pit pony manure heap and there are lots of field voles in the rough grass about the railway lines and the canal banks. Farmed land is no use to a barn owl. You won't tell anybody about this, Eddie? You won't tell anybody?'

'No. Of course not.'

'It's our secret, then?'

'Look here, Lawrence. Who would I want to tell about you coming between my legs?'

'Oh,' Lawrence laughed. 'I don't mean *that!* I couldn't give a sod about it. I meant the barn owls. It's the barn owls that's secret. Pull your trousers up. We'd best be off.'

They repeated the visit – and the action Lawrence couldn't give a sod about – several times. Then the onset of bad weather brought an end to their pleasure. The mating season was over.

CHAPTER TWO

Edward pulled his knitted balaclava helmet tighter to his face. The searing east wind caused his eyes to water. He pressed his back harder against the playground wall as if the brickwork itself might offer some warmth. In order to stop his teeth chattering, he decided to shuffle across the yard. He had no idea where the hands came from, but he felt them dig into the small of his back and pitch him forward on to the wet slush and snow. He picked himself up, his fingers numb with cold, his jacket and trousers wet, and strode purposefully forward.

'You can't go into the classroom. We ain't allowed inside.'

A thin, pathetic boy called Malcolm Cattermole stood shivering in the entrance to the main building. He wore only a jersey over the top of his short trousers. He had forgotten his coat and was in fear of the consequences of going inside to get it. In spite of the fact that Malcolm wiped his snotty nose on his sleeve, wore glasses and had a sickly smell about him, Eddie liked Malcolm and would chat to him from time to time when most boys wouldn't give him the time of day. As Eddie was the closest to a friend that Malcolm had got, Malcolm revered his cleverness where others scoffed at it.

'You'll get stick if you go in,' Malcolm warned.

'I'm not going in the classroom, am I? I'm going into

the cloakroom. Nobody has said we can't go in there, have they?'

Eddie's reassurance must have given Malcolm either confidence or courage for he trailed behind the younger boy. On the way in, Eddie turned swiftly to the left and darted into the classroom, snatched his library book from beneath his desk and made his way out to the cloakroom. Open-mouthed, Malcolm observed Eddie's flagrant disobedience. Eddie wasn't normally one to flout rules. Malcolm was even more amazed when he saw Eddie seat himself comfortably on top of the cloakroom hot water pipes.

'We're not in the classroom, are we?' Eddie opened his book and the steam began to rise from his trousers.

'Any pictures in it?' Malcolm nodded in the direction of Eddie's book.

'Only three,' Eddie replied judiciously. 'It's exciting, though.'

'I expect it's all long words. Do you want to read to us?' Malcolm's question was more of an appeal.

'Of course. If you want. *Then at dusk he had got on his camel and ridden off to the railway with the few mounted men to fight. The two hundred infantry determined to do its duty against the landing party: but they were outnumbered three to one, and the naval gunfire was too heavy to let them make proper use of their positions . . .*'

'You! You boys! Out. Out of there. No, not outside. Classroom first. What were you doing in there?'

Eddie's teacher never seemed to waste many words. Most of his working day was spent giving orders rather than explanation or instruction. His classroom techniques were wholly based on fear. He liked to think it was respect. Teaching skills were something he felt he could do without. He was a great believer in common sense. He was always asking his students to use it. Any trace of imagination or creativity he would have regarded as being close to blasphemy.

When they reached the classroom, Eddie attempted to answer his question.

'I was just reading, sir, and Malcolm was listening. We were just warming our hands . . .'

Eddie's words died on the air. His teacher did not appear to be listening. He had opened the cupboard and was reaching behind a row of dust-covered ancient Bibles stacked on the back of the shelf.

'Warming your hands, were you?' He spoke with his back to them and turned to face them armed with a thick cane that had some adhesive tape bound around its end. 'If your hands were cold, I'd better warm them up for you.' He said nothing more to them but nodded his head for Malcolm to step forward.

Eddie watched the ugly ritual, fascinated and trans-fixed with horror. This man smiled at Malcolm before he began his performance. He tested the torture instru-ment's pliability, bending it just one way and then another.

'Hold out your hand. Left first. You'll remember right from left after this, boy.'

He flicked the back of Malcolm's outstretched hand with the cane so that the boy's palm could be extended in just the right position. On such matters, this man was a perfectionist. The blow was swift but fierce. Three more blows followed. Two strokes on either hand. As the fourth blow fell, Malcolm cried out in pain. Instead of leaving the room, he lingered behind and waited for Eddie. The teacher seemed to be too preoccupied with his duties to notice his presence.

Eddie extended his arm and held out his hand. He closed his eyes and clenched his teeth. He felt the cane on the back of his hand flicking it higher than his shoulder.

'You'll be leaving us soon then, boy?'

'Yes, sir. In four days' time . . . ah! . . . ah! . . . ah!'

The first blow crashed across his fingers and caused him to cry out. He would speak no more to this man. Rotten swine. Dirty bugger. Shit pig. Never. Another blow followed. The third stroke seemed to tear the ends of Eddie's fingers. Barely conscious, he suffered the fourth and final blow. He felt sick. He bent forward and held both hands underneath his armpits as if hiding the source of the pain might somehow banish it.

'Well, there's a little something to remember us by.' The man spoke as he returned the cane to its holy resting place behind the Bibles.

'Don't let him see you cry,' Malcolm whispered.

'What was that, Cattermole?'

'Nothing, sir. I didn't say nothing.'

'Oh. You didn't say nothing.'

'He never spoke. He never said anything,' Eddie muttered.

'Are you calling me a liar, Warrington? There is no wax in my ears.'

Pain had somehow exorcised Eddie's fear.

'He groaned, sir. It was a groan you heard.' Eddie stared at the man with a fixed, glazed intent. This teacher was not used to such a level of anger and hostility from a juvenile. Momentarily, his self-willed power wavered.

'Out. Out!' he shouted at the two boys, who then lost no time in getting out of the hell hole that was called a classroom.

Eddie took no part in the afternoon lessons. Composition and dictation were ignored. He couldn't hold a pen in his hand, let alone write with one. He sat at his desk and read page after page of his library book, from time to time staring openly at his teacher in silent loathing. For some reason, the man chose not to meet Eddie's gaze or question his inactivity. For his part, Eddie ruminated over the injustice of his wounds and knew that he would never forgive the man.

'Proctor is a shit-bag. If I had a gun I'd shoot him up the arse. Slowly.'

'It's not possible to fire a gun slowly.' Eddie brought sound reasoning to Malcolm's pronouncement but did not disagree with the sentiments his friend had expressed. They parted company at the corner of the street. Injury and pain had brought them almost to the verge of close friendship.

'I'll see you tomorrow then, Eddie,' Malcolm spoke as if he might even be looking forward to the event.

'It's Saturday tomorrow,' Eddie smiled as he answered.

By the time he had hung up his coat and filled the coal bucket, Eddie felt he ought to have been able to forget about the caning, but he could not. For some reason, he felt a deep sense of shame. His hands were still sore but they no longer throbbed with pain.

He now obeyed his mother unquestioningly when she asked him to peel the potatoes. He was usually prone to grumbling in such circumstances. He had never received a great deal of affection from her and in turn had hardly ever been a dutiful boy. The task proved difficult; his injuries had left him momentarily clumsy and unnerved.

'What did you do? Did you give anyone cheek?' His mother's eagle eyes rarely missed much. Yet like most predatory birds, she appeared indifferent in repose. She had struck quickly, without warning. She had seized his wrists and was now glaring down at his damaged hands. Her mouth twitched with rage.

'I was given four strokes. Two on each hand.'

'What the bloody hell did he hit you with? A plank?' She frowned and shook her head. 'Well? What did you do wrong?'

Eddie truthfully related the gravity of his misdemeanour. She grunted but said nothing more about the matter.

His father's homecoming followed its usual ritual. On arrival, he hung his pit helmet and knapsack behind a door which led under the staircase to nowhere. When he was a small child, Eddie's mother had always referred to it as a *bogey hole* and, to some extent, Eddie still saw it in that light. This narrow room had once been used for storing coal inside the house. It was now a dark space which held his mother's rug-making materials. The outside of the door had been used as a darts board and was scarred with tiny holes. The inside was studded with large nails. This part of the door was Eddie's father's pit wardrobe. A cane also hung there.

Eddie looked on as his mother poured out his father's tea and began a tirade before the poor man had taken his first sip. The pit grime seemed to enhance his physical exhaustion. He had taken his teeth out. Red-eyed, toothless, he appeared older than his years. He began to look stricken as Eddie's mother regaled him with the source of Eddie's injuries.

'Mam. Mam. Don't blame my dad. It's not fair. You can't . . .' Eddie tried to interrupt as he felt his mother was making it seem as though it were his dad's fault that he had been caned.

'Shut up, you. You've always got too much to say for yourself. I'm not talking to you, am I?' she snapped at Eddie.

His father held up his hand, indicating that she should cease talking. He never interrupted or shouted over her. She paused and listened to him.

'Look. There are rules everywhere. I don't agree with all of them but I get on with it. I have to do things down there under the ground that I don't like doing. Everybody has a gaffer, and the gaffer makes the rules. And that's that.'

'No, it's not bloody that!' She banged on the table with her fist. 'If your gaffer did to you what that . . . that *creature* has done to our Eddie, I'd be down at the pit. Look at his bloody hands. Look at the state of them! You've never laid a hand on him yourself and you sit there and tell me it's alright for other people to do what you won't do. And what was he lashed for? For staying in out of the cold. I wouldn't be surprised if half those kids don't come down with the soddin' 'flu or pneumonia. I wouldn't have let a dog outside today, let alone kids.'

'I never said he should have hit Eddie.'

'No, but you're doing bugger all about it. Well, I am. I'm at that school on Monday. If that man lays a finger on him again, I'll swing for what I'll do for him. If Eddie's bad, then they can tell me and I'll cane him. You won't. I will. I had him; I'll be the judge and jury if they are needed.'

'Well that's that, then,' Eddie's father sounded relieved.

'Is it?' she asked.

'I don't want you to go up to the school,' Eddie murmured.

'It's none of your business. Come and eat your dinners. Both of you. It's my business. It has to be.'

Eddie had little appetite for the fried onions in Bisto gravy and the slice of white bread.

'Eat it,' his mother commanded.

'It's good. It's very good.' His father nodded as he dipped his bread into the gravy. This dual onslaught of direction and encouragement helped Eddie to leave his plate clean.

Eddie sat quietly at his desk. It was Monday and it was two pm. By now the day had lost its tension; she wouldn't call now. If his mother had called in on the class, he had decided that he would disown her. He and his classmates were embroiled in handwriting exercises that they must have done scores of times before. The collective boredom had produced a torpor within the room almost as effectively as chloroform. Eddie relaxed as he made a long series of the letter g. Just as he moved on to the letter h, the classroom door opened. His mother, for that was who it was, closed it quietly behind her.

Eddie was pleased to see she had on her best green coat, the one with the brown velvet collar. She wore her high heels and stockings, even the hat with feathers on the side that she'd only worn once, for his Uncle Johnny's wedding. She had her gloves on, and she had some powder and lipstick on her face.

Mr Proctor came from behind his desk as though he were greeting an important visitor. He had never met Eddie's mother before so he couldn't possibly know who this lady was, or why she was here. All the boys let their pens lie still and watched as the high-heeled shoes clopped to a tidy halt when they had reached the middle of the wooden floor space.

'Can I help you, madam?' Proctor's voice boomed with an air of false courtesy.

He doesn't like women, Eddie thought. *Even if he is married. He doesn't like them like my father does.*

'No, there's no way you can help me at all.' Eddie's mother knew all about condescension. She spoke sharply and fearlessly and looked at Mr Proctor in the same way as he looked at his pupils. Without respect.

'I beg your pardon?'

'You can beg all day and night but you'll get no pardon from me. Not even if you were on your hands and knees.'

'Who are you, may I ask?'

'I am Esther Warrington, Eddie's mother.' She nodded in Eddie's direction as she said this, acknowledging her offspring as though his birth had been a major achievement. Eddie felt quite proud and not in any way uncomfortable.

There was a wobble in Mr Proctor's voice that none of the class had heard before.

'I think you had better make your way to the headmaster's study, Mrs Warrington. Turn left and walk straight down the corridor, then turn right and it is right at the very end. The door is marked.'

'So are my son's hands. I don't want to see the headmaster. It's you I've come to see. Lay a finger on Eddie ever again and I'll swing for you. As God's my judge, I will.'

'You can't come in here like this and . . .'

'Can't? *Can't*? I've done, haven't I? Touch him again and I'll have your number, even if it sees me in hospital or jail. There. That's it.' She turned to Eddie. 'You have two more days here.' She glanced at the rows of letters on the blackboard. 'You'll attend to your lessons – such as they are. You were doing this in infants' school.'

Her case stated, she clopped her way out and closed the door softly behind her. Eddie had never known the class so quiet. Nobody even sniffed or coughed.

'Get on with your handwriting.' Mr Proctor's voice still had a wobble in it.

For the rest of the afternoon, all that could be heard was the scratching noise of pen nibs on paper and the occasional sigh from boys who took no joy in their labours or the outcome of the results.

The following afternoon Eddie had answered the registration call. There were three Ws and one Y. Mr Proctor pressed the blotting pad firmly on the page and closed the book. His roll-call was always slow and thorough and if a boy failed to answer clearly enough he would bawl at them, 'Speak properly, boy, when you answer. And say "sir" so that I can hear it.'

When Malcolm came in, Mr Proctor turned and looked up at the clock behind him.

'It's after half past one, Cattermole.' All the class looked up. The dreaded minute finger was closer to the seven than the six. 'No. Don't sit down, boy. Remain where you are at the front of the class.'

'I'm sorry I'm late, sir. It's not my fault. I'm to tell you—'

'I don't want any excuses, boy ...' Mr Proctor had already opened the cupboard door and had extended his arm to reach for the cane.

'My mother's not well, sir. I had to get my little sister into school first and she wouldn't walk quickly enough. My mam said I was to tell you.'

Mr Proctor seemed deaf to this plea for leniency and stepped forward with the cane.

'Hold out your hand, boy.'

Malcolm did not respond to this order, but remained mute with his hands pressed firmly against the sides of his trousers.

'Hold out your hand, boy.'

Once again, Malcolm ignored the request. He shook his head from side to side in a slow, deliberate denial.

'No, sir. No. I won't. My mother says I'm not to. She says I'm not to take any more stick from you.'

The class was enthralled with the unfolding drama.

Their lesson time had rarely held excitement or even interest. This was a cracking way to spend the afternoon. Opposition of this kind had never been witnessed before and Malcolm Cattermole had no previous record for courage.

'Come on, now. Let's have no more of this cissy, namby-pamby business, Cattermole. Take your punishment like a man.'

Eddie watched the fingers of Malcolm's right hand move slightly away from his trouser pocket. He sensed that Malcolm's determination was weakening. When he saw Malcolm's hand move, Eddie spoke out. He spoke out clearly so that everyone could hear.

'He's not a man, he's a boy. You've said so yourself, sir. If he were a man, you would not dare hit him.'

As if obeying some signal, Malcolm crossed his arms across his chest and clamped each hand under his armpits. Rather than prolong his defeat, Mr Proctor chose to defuse this disobedience with a short burst of sarcasm.

'Oh, sit down. Go to your seat. There's no football for you this afternoon. You can go and play ring-a-ring-a-roses at the girls' school instead.' He was hoping for sniggers or laughter from the class to support this jibe, but the boys sat in silent support of Malcolm. 'You, boy!' Mr Proctor pointed toward Edward. 'Out. Outside the classroom. And you can stay there until home time. Then you can go back to your mother's apron strings.'

Edward was no longer afraid of Mr Proctor. He was glad to be leaving the classroom. What was more, he knew that he would never have to return to it again. He opened his desk lid and carefully stored his exercise books away, then he removed a reading book from the bottom and closed the lid.

'Leave that, boy. Leave that book where it is,' Proctor commanded.

'It belongs to me. It's from the Central Library. My mother wants it at home. I have to return it tomorrow.'

'Oh, well. You'd better do as mummy tells you, hadn't you?'

Edward got up from his desk as Malcolm sat down behind his.

'My mother and Malcolm's mother are much more like men than you are supposed to be, Mr Proctor. My mother drove a crane at the factory all night long and Malcolm's mother loaded shell cases, and they have never been afraid of people like you. Never.'

'Out! Out!' Mr Proctor roared as if he were going to explode with rage.

Edward left the room quietly but before he had closed the door the laughter had started. All the boys were laughing at Mr Proctor and there was nothing he could do about it. Edward smiled to himself and sniffed an unusual type of satisfaction that verged on exhilaration. The feeling was new to him.

'Now he's got something to remember *me* by,' he muttered to a world of people he was yet to meet.

CHAPTER THREE

'Aren't you going out? It's Sunday night. You ought to be getting ready. It's past seven. Aren't you going out?'

Edward's mother sat close to the fire stabbing holes in hessian potato sacking with a wooden peg that had been sharpened to a point. She worked swiftly with great deftness and, if it were not for the glorious patterning revealed on the other side of the rug, one might have thought her work was automatic and without skill. She took a long time before speaking, picking through the right bits of cloth with her fingers. Edward had often accused her of deafness with regard to her late responses to his questioning.

'I want to finish this. I'll take it into Batsford with me on Monday. I took an order for it last week. The woman's calling in for it in the afternoon. A well-to-do woman, she is. You'd have thought she could have afforded a carpet.'

'They look better than carpets. You don't charge enough for them. Perhaps you might finish it by nine.'

She looked up from her work and sighed.

'No, Edward, I won't be finished by nine. Do you think I'm a bloody octopus? I won't be going out tonight. I've told your father he's at the club on his own. I'm staying in tonight, so you've got me for company and you'll have to like it and lump it. Switch the wireless on. It's Wilfred Pickles in a few seconds.'

Edward put on his overcoat and scarf as soon as the *Have A Go* signature tune and chorus belted out its message over the airwaves. He loathed the programme as much as his mother enjoyed it.

'And where do you think you're going? You're too late for the pictures.'

'I'm going up to my bedroom.'

'Bedrooms are for sleeping in, not for sitting around in.'

'I'll read. I can't read down here with that stuff on the wireless.'

She shrugged her shoulders and said, 'Please yourself.' Edward knew that this had nothing to do with pleasing anyone. She should have said, 'I don't care what you do.' It would have been nearer the truth. 'And don't start singing and gazing into the mirror. One of these days your reflection will answer you back!'

Even in summer, the two bedrooms in the house were cold. At this time of year, the temperature in them was close to freezing. Sometimes Edward had watched as his own breath was visible on the air when he released small puffs from his parted lips. All the houses in the row, and there were twelve of them, were well past improvement. The roofs leaked. The rooms were damp and cold. There was no bathroom, no hot water and there were six outside toilets between twelve households, situated in an outhouse at the bottom of the back yard. They were condemned verbally by all who lived in them, yet defended by the same people if they came under attack from anyone else.

'There's many who would be glad to have a roof over their head.'

'Winning a war seems to have done sod all for me,' his mother had spoken with some bitterness after she and many of the women who worked alongside her at the factory were laid off work. After being told to work for the war effort, they were now being exhorted to return to the womanly delights of the kitchen and romantic domesticity. 'I can't stay here all day. I've got a job three days a week on a market stall in Batsford. The woollens and baby stall. Everybody seems in the family way. I hear Leah Jenkins is having another one. She's forty-four. God Almighty! Talk about making up for lost time.'

There was nothing personalised about Edward's bedroom. It contained linoleum, a bed, a wardrobe and a dressing table. There was one picture, of a shaggy-looking bull standing in miles of mountainous purple heather, aptly titled *Lost In The Glen*. Edward hung his scarf over the forlorn looking creature after he had closed his bedroom door.

No matter how bleak the surroundings, privacy still constituted a form of luxury. Within limits, he could do what he wanted to do and say what he felt like saying. He sat on his bed and faced the dressing table mirror. First he'd write a letter. He loved receiving the answers to these letters and referred to them to his mother as his *correspondence*.

Taking the cardboard case from the wardrobe he looked through the wonderful array of replies. They were all picture postcards and they had been sent to him all the way from the United States of America. Katharine Hepburn. Ricardo Montalban. Gregory Peck. Lana Turner. Jennifer Jones. He leafed through this pile of photographic treasure and chose three of them to keep him company. Now, as he looked at himself in the mirror, he also had the company of Greer Garson, Tyrone Power and his latest acquisition, Farley Grainger. He was all set to write a note to Sterling Hayden, but couldn't really think of why he wanted the picture of him.

He put his pencil on the bed and looked from the photos in front of him and back to himself. His black curls topped a wide brow, his dark brown eyes were soft and spaniel-like, the complexion pale and the lips full. It was not an unpleasing face, but he couldn't fall in love with it. He could never really believe it was him that he was looking at. So it was easy to converse with it.

'When I wrote to Greer Garson, I should have said *I wish you were my mother instead of the one I've got*. I didn't say that. I said, *I loved your performances in Mrs Miniver and Valley of Decision*. And why did I write to Tyrone Power when I can't stand sword-fighting pictures? I honestly don't know why I sent off for Farley Grainger. Boys don't have pin-up pictures of boys. I'm not allowed to stick any pictures up, but it's wonderful to think that all these stars are here with me in this room. My dad says our village is the dead centre of England. Centre of England or not, I want to leave it just as soon as I'm old enough. I don't want to live here. I want to fall in love but I don't want to be noticed.

'In the last few months I've learned how babies are got. I know I never want to make one with a girl. My mam and dad told me great lies about all this. He'd laugh and say *We found you under a gooseberry bush*. She said *Nurse Wainwright brought you to us in a little black bag. Had you placed an order for me*? I asked her. *No, no. You were a mistake. She wouldn't take you back, so I've got to make the best of it*. She meant this. I know she did. She's never kissed me. She's never even put her arm around me, I don't think. I don't think she's ever wanted to touch me. He did – my dad did – when I was little. He'd take my hand. But not her. She could never be Mrs Miniver.'

Edward placed Greer Garson and Tyrone Power back

in the case and was left with Farley Grainger. The charming smile and kindly eyes seemed to be speaking gently just to him. Edward brought his lips to within an inch or two of the mirror and whispered, 'Oh Farley! Take me in your arms!'

'Edward? Edward!' his mother called from the bottom of the stairs. 'What are you doing up there?'

'I'm writing to Sterling Hayden,' Edward shouted back in exasperation.

'Who the hell is that?' Her response was equally short. 'With that light on up there you're burning money. It's finished now.'

'The rug. You've finished it? You're going out?'

'No. No. Not the rug. Wilfred Pickles is finished. You can listen to the play or Radio Luxembourg and cut some cloth for me. Now just you get your legs down here before I come up and fetch you down. Come down and switch that light off. We can't afford to burn money.'

It was more pleasant cutting the cloth into strips and listening to Jo Stafford singing about someone she loved who was in jail than Edward thought it might be. His mother worked furiously. She would pause only to take a drag from her Woodbine then balance it back on the fender. In the past he had taunted her by singing *Smoke Gets in Your Eyes*.

'If you sing that once more, you'll get my hand across your face, you little snipe.'

But tonight a truce had been called. It was as if the two of them had been plonked on a desert island and they'd had to make the best of it, like the Swiss Family Robinson did.

'Don't cut any more. I've enough here. Just this last bit of edging to do.' She did not look but continued to work as she spoke. And then, with a small degree of satisfaction or relief rather than triumph. 'There. It's done. It's finished. Oh God, it's past ten. Your dad will be here in a few minutes. Help me spread it out.'

'It's lovely, Mam,' Edward declared. 'Can't we keep it?'

'It's sold. It's sold already. I've told you. We can't live on air, you know. Get the other end. Help me roll it up. I've got to lug this into Batsford tomorrow. There'll be no joy in getting on the bus with this.'

'I can come with you. I'll help you with it.'

'You've got school. I'll be on the quarter to nine bus.'

'I don't have to go tomorrow. We'll be doing nothing anyway. It's the day before half-term – my last day there – I won't be missed.'

'Don't you want to say ta-ra to your friends?'

'I've already done that. I could go to the library after you get to the stall. I'm supposed to read a book called *Ivanhoe* and a history book about the Tudors. It says so in my letter from my new school.'

Edward's mother shook her head as she knelt on the floor and looked at Edward, who was in a similar posture, bent over the rug. She laughed, 'You crafty little bugger. When did you work all that out? I sometimes wish our dad had some of your guile. He's as honest as the day is long, and suffers for it. Alright, then. Don't mention it to your dad because I can tell you he won't like it.'

'Do you love him?'

'Who?'

'My dad.'

'I'm married to him, aren't I?'

'I don't think you love him enough. I think if you—'

'There, I can hear him opening the yard gate. Why don't you ask him when he comes in. Just see how far you'll get with such squitch. Ask him. Ask him when he comes in.'

'Shush, Mam. Shush. I was only joking.'

His father came in and placed a bottle of milk stout on the sideboard.

'There you are, Esther. Drink that and it'll do you good. Our Alice and our Jack asked after you at the club. Mrs Franklin sang a few songs. I don't think much of her voice. It's strong but it's harsh.'

'She thinks she's Vera Lynn. She's done more than sing to soldiers in her time.' Edward's mother got up from the floor while she talked and transferred the bottle of stout to the table.

'Yes, we all missed you, Esther.'

'Did you?' She took a Woodbine from the pack of cigarettes and smiled triumphantly at Edward before she lit it.

The next day, Edward sat on the bus beside his mother, the rug stretched across their laps. In spite of this cumbersome arrangement, Edward was glad of the coverage. At the most inconvenient times nowadays his cock would seem to develop a will of its own. As the bus bumped and hauled itself along the crater-scarred road, it reared up like a traffic indicator. Matters worsened as the uncircumcised head of his dick rubbed and pressed at the rough cloth of his trousers.

If I was in bed, I could toss off.

Like most boys in his locality, Edward attached no guilt to this activity. Sister Bessie, the deaconess of the Bethany Baptist Chapel had caught two boys at it behind the shutters at the Wednesday night youth club. She'd gone purple in the face and told them they could go mad if they did it and end up in a loony bin, or worse, their heads would face round the wrong way if they did it again. Anyway, they had done it scores of times since then and they weren't in the loony bin and their heads were still the right way round.

Just a week ago in the middle of sorting out the wash for the boiler, his mother had drawn attention to the hard, encrusted semen stain on his pyjama trousers.

'Oh God. These will need to be boiled.' Edward had felt the blood rush to his face but she was not concerned with his embarrassment and seemed totally unaffected. 'Put a handkerchief in your pyjama pocket before you got to bed. It will save your pyjamas and the sheets.' Eddie had merely half-coughed and grunted in response. 'Thank God in Heaven you're not a girl. It would be blood by now. I think nature is far from fair.' She had laughed and added, 'Just like love.'

What had she meant, *blood*? He had heard some older boys at school saying that their sisters *had the rags on*. Did this mean they had to wear cloth inside their knickers? And did all women have to have them on? How did it feel to be without a dick? And why did some boys go to any lengths to have a glance at a girl's knickers and why was . . .?

His mother nudged him sharply in the ribs with her elbow.

'Come on, Edward. We're here. You'd day-dream your life away, given half a chance.' Edward's mother never appeared to set much store by contemplation, even in her moments of reflection, her hands were busy knitting or rug-making. She was rarely still. 'You take the back,' she ordered and they made their way through the town in this fashion until they reached the stall in the market square. Edward felt the journey was reminiscent of Jack and the Beanstalk in some ways but pantomime had disappointed him and his mother's strictures for the day ahead left him no further time for conjecture on the matter.

'Now here's a penny for your bus fare home and a threepenny bit for you to get a bag of chips for your dinner. See that you are in the house when your dad gets in, by half-past four. Have the coal bucket filled and give him his cup of tea when he's sat himself down. And don't talk his head off, you hear?'

'I'm not deaf, Mam.'

'No, but you can talk the hind leg off a donkey and a man wants a bit of peace and quiet when he gets home from work. What are you going to do if they haven't got your books at the library?'

'They will have them. Miss Gayle is getting them for me. She always gets the books I want.'

'I was at school with her, you know, Eddie. Clever girl. She was always going to be a maid, though. Lives in a bungalow with Olive Goodman who drives an ambulance at Stafford Hospital. If Angela Gayle had been a man, she'd be in charge of that library, not second in command. I've always liked her. And Olive.'

'She likes you, Mam. She said so.'

'Not half as much as she likes you, our Edward. You're about the only male I know who's ever taken her fancy.'

'Why didn't she marry? Was her boyfriend killed in the war?' Edward was anxious to weave romance about one of his heroines.

'No. She's never had a boyfriend. It wouldn't have been natural for her.' An abrupt change of tone indicated that any further conversation would be unnecessary and that time had been wasted in an exchange of words. 'Talk talk talk. You'd go on until the cows came home. Off you go. Remember what I've told you.'

There was one long main square to the town of Batsford, and apart from the four public houses, the market and a few shops down the side roads which led from it, there was little else. The square itself was imposing enough. Standing in one corner was the

Norman-built parish church of St Chad's, surrounded by great lawns and fruit trees which were never plundered by a populace who would have derived a great deal of benefit from the vitamins the fruit had to offer. Along the centre of the square there were testaments of aesthetic interest to the people who meandered about. There was a clock, whose face was perched on a tall Doric plinth. It was reliable only in that the time fingers had read it to be a quarter past eleven ever since Edward could remember. His father had an affection for it.

'They say time waits for no man, but our clock in Batsford does.'

Eddie had often wondered what had caused it to stop, and whether it had gone wonky at night or in the morning. Further along stood four bronze soldiers. One looked up to the sky as he held what looked like a flagpole in both hands. The other three were grouped about him in a *pietà*-like pose, as though they were witnessing some new crucifixion. Edward had often looked down the list of names on this First World War memorial and now saw that a much smaller, and less prepossessing piece of statuary had been placed at the feet of the soldiers. This was a large stone open book which commemorated the war Edward himself had known. Carved on the top, it read *Roll of Honour* but the open pages remained blank as the names had not yet been added. Edward reflected that he'd rather have his name stuck up in front of the picture house than on a war memorial, as people took more notice of it.

This town was the centre of his universe, its population swollen by the several rural and mining villages that were dotted about it. The region, strangely isolated by its position, had an excess of young men. After the war, Bevin boys had left the collieries for their own homes and regions. The ranks of returning miners had been swelled, however, by migrant Polish and Lithuanian refugees who had been granted a status here so long as they remained at the coal face for a period of time. Some of these men were always to be seen talking in groups of three or four. No-one understood them but people would smile and nod.

Some nine miles from the town, a huge RAF camp had been thrown up on a bleak, harsh piece of chase land, surrounded by pine forests, to cater for three thousand young men involved in doing their compulsory National Service. For most of these eighteen to twenty year olds, Batsford was the centre of civilisation. They would walk round and round the square, homesick, penniless, sporting uniforms which they would prefer not to wear. Unless a young girl was hopelessly backward or terribly handicapped, she could be assured of marriage in Batsford if she so desired. The plainest, fattest girls were normally in bridal white before they were twenty-one and most of them had babies within a year. They started to go from schoolgirls to married women in next to no time at all.

CHAPTER FOUR

'I'll see to Edward, Pauline. You take your break now, dear. It's half past ten. You might want to do a little shopping in the town. You can finish the cataloguing when you get back. Alright, dear?' Angela Gayle's brisk, pleasant manner towards her assistant changed to one of an elder sister's affection when she turned to greet Edward. 'I have your books, Edward. Also a little gift for you.'

Vindictive tongues might at times refer to Angela as an old maid, but to Edward's viewing, she hardly looked the part. She was a tall woman of very slim appearance and insignificant bosom. As far as clothing was concerned, Angela did not favour the greys, the warmed-out pale greens, the fawns, the beiges that professional women of her standing usually wore. Today she wore a bright, pillar-box red pleated skirt with a multicoloured Fair Isle patterned pullover. Just below her right shoulder a shiny, silvery brooch sparkled in the shape of a cat. Most women of her age were soft-permed or frizzed but Angela had never had her tresses cooked. Her thick, bright blonde hair (some said the colour came out of a bottle) fell in a sharp, level fringe over her wide brow. The rest was braided into one long, fat plait with a red ribbon tied neatly at the end of it. This appendage fascinated Edward as one never knew whether it would hang over Angela's right shoulder, her left one or trail half-way down her back. She wore orange-red lipstick, dabs of rouge on her high cheeks and pencilled light brown, highly arched eyebrows which gave her small, kindly blue eyes a look of permanent surprise. Her wrists were never without a bracelet and she wore a small signet ring with a black stone in it on the little finger of her right hand. Her perfume, which had a strong floral base, was called *June*. She replenished this on her person throughout the day and people truthfully observed that you could often smell Angela before you saw her. Edward adored her and Angela was not a woman who would reject a fan.

She placed the books on the counter.

'You've brought your father's ticket with you?' Edward nodded. 'Good. There is an extra book on the Tudors. Social history. Most important, I think. Social history is concerned with the ordinary people and how they lived and worked. People like us.'

'I don't think you are ordinary, Miss Gayle,' Edward stated this honestly, not meaning to flatter or be sycophantic. Angela Gayle sighed audibly.

'I wonder if our history will ever be written – yours and mine?'

Edward didn't quite know what had caused her to sigh. Was it that she and Edward weren't ordinary enough? Or was it that they would never achieve any significant recordable fame?

'Here's your copy of *Ivanhoe* and this book gives a critical assessment of three of Sir Walter Scott's novels, one of which is your set book. Do read the novel before the criticism. A fish never tastes so good if you dissect it before you've sniffed its aroma. Olive and I are thrilled about you getting your grammar school place. I suppose you're looking forward to it.'

'Yes. I am. I'm longing to get started there.'

'It's been an exciting time for me, too, Edward.' Angela leaned forward, lifted her plait from behind her neck and plonked it over her left shoulder. She had lowered her voice and now spoke in hushed, confidential tones. 'After months – *months* of meetings, discussions, notes and endless discourse with mindless, Philistine, locally elected councillors, after months of cajoling, soft-soaping and yes sir no sir three bags full sir exchanges, I have finally got my way.'

'What's happened, Miss Gayle?' Edward was more than curious. The rapturous smile and blissful countenance of Angela caused Edward to think that she was going to put up to stand for Parliament or had at least got herself a job working in the top flight of the county council. He was pleased for her. She ruled Batsford Library but when all was said and done, the place was only a very long, windowless oblong wooden shed painted dark green on the outside and lined with books from within.

'I'll show you, Edward. Follow me.' Angela made no attempt to keep the tones of self-satisfaction from her voice. 'This way.' She beckoned him to follow her as she emerged from behind the counter and strode purposefully past the volumes of books which she cared for and tended and none of which gave her any representation either in fact or fiction.

At the bottom end a narrow door, newly hacked out of the woodwork, declared its birth. Pinned on to this was a white piece of card with black lettering on it which spelt out REFERENCE LIBRARY. Miss Gayle paused in front of it in a most reverential way as if she were in a church taking a bit of bread or a sip of wine.

'There. There! Batsford has a reference library. Go in, Edward. Go in. You will be the first person to use it. Go in. Lift up the latch.'

Edward felt as if he had been asked to christen a ship instead of opening a wooden side door to the library, but he realised it was all so important to Miss Gayle and knew that if he entered her enthusiasm, she would feel even better. It was like feeling sorry for someone backwards. He purposefully made the latch click as loudly as possible and opened the door more slowly than doors were opened in Frankenstein films.

'Oh, Miss Gayle, how *wonderful*,' Edward cooed as if he were staring at some vast hidden treasure, long secreted from the eyes of men. In fact he looked into a garden shed with a small window placed too high for anyone to look out of. There were two tables and eight chairs filling most of its space, and a sign which read

THIS ROOM REQUIRES <u>SILENCE</u>

with the word 'silence' underlined. Edward stepped forward and sat down on one of the chairs, placed his books on the table, opened one of them, rested his elbow on the table, cupped his chin in his hands and mimed the muse of study.

'Oh, Edward, I wish I had a camera,' Angela fluttered on. 'I forgot to give you something. Wait there. Stay where you are,' she commanded.

Edward was unused to presents. His birthday was within a few days of Christmas and for the past four years, his mother had said a new pair of shoes, a pair of long trousers or a raincoat constituted his Christmas *and* birthday present. There was never any element of surprise in the matter. So when Angela returned with a small parcel furled in gaudy green wrapping paper, he felt almost overcome and even speechless. To be at a loss for words was rare for him.

She placed it on the table before him.

'Well, Edward. Aren't you going to open it? It won't open itself, you know. It's from Olive and me.'

'Now? I can open it now?' Edward had already begun to finger the wrapping paper as he spoke and as Angela Gayle nodded, he carefully levered the paper away from the box within it. On the cream cardboard box a swan nestled amongst some bulrushes and nestled inside the box, as if they were eggs from some rare bird, lay a maroon-coloured fountain pen and pencil set.

'Oh, Miss Gayle! It's just what I need. It's very kind of you – er – and your friend, Olive. The colour will match my blazer. I've never had a fountain pen before. Thank you ever so much.'

'I thought it would be nice for you to have something to remember me by.'

'But I'm not going away, Miss Gayle. I shall still come in here and see you.'

Edward meant this. If ever he were rich or famous, he'd buy her and Olive magnificent evening dresses to wear. Such was the extent of his gratitude, it never occurred to him that both women would look distinctly odd in organza or yards of chiffon.

Miss Gayle lifted the pen from its box.

'I'll fill this for you. Perhaps you can try it out here.' She paused as some fresh intelligence occurred to her. 'Indeed, I wonder if you could do something to help me in the next hour or so.' She glanced at her wristwatch. 'No. Forty-five minutes.'

'Whatever you like. I'll do whatever you like, Miss Gayle.'

'Well, Edward, I'd like you to sit in here. I'll give you some notepaper and, er, if you would read and study with great intensity when I bring the visitors in, it could help me a great deal.'

'Visitors?'

38

'Three members of the local council, who like to see how their money is spent. I tell you, Edward, if the arts, culture and public enlightenment were left to some people, we would be back to barbarism within a decade. They should be here in thirty or forty minutes. You won't let me down? I can count on you? You don't want to go to the toilet, do you?'

'Trust me, Miss Gayle.' Edward turned to the beginning of *Ivanhoe* with the expected intensity of purpose as he spoke.

Edward found the novel easy to assimilate and he loved the names of the characters, like Rowena and Brian de Bois Guilbert. In fact, he was used to reading books of a much more adult nature. Volatile, passionate books about slave girls in the Deep South by Frank Yerby, *Forever Amber* by Kathleen Windsor and such like. The closest he'd got to enjoying children's books were *She* and *Alan Quartermaine* by Rider Haggard, *The Swiss Family Robinson* and North American Indian books by Fenimore Cooper. He had found all children's literature like the *Doctor Dolittle* books of no interest whatsoever.

Ivanhoe soon had his attention but he felt gravely discomfited and hoped the visitors would arrive sooner rather than later. His mild attack of claustrophobia was not centered in the content of the book before, but from the air about him. The freshly erected wooden walls seemed to ooze creosote. The smell seemed to be all about and instead of fading, it seemed to be increasing in its pungency the longer he sat there. He tried to close his nostrils to it but this was impossible. He breathed through his mouth but the fumes and his vivid imagination began to make him feel nauseous.

'I'm not in Belsen or Dachau. I'm only in Batsford. It's not a Nazi gas chamber, it's only a reference library.'

He repeated phrases like this over and over again in order to stop himself from leaving this prison to gulp some fresh air. He'd rather die than let Miss Gayle down.

At the very point where he felt he might well achieve such a sacrifice, the latch clicked.

'Ah, Edward, you are in here. I hadn't expected our reference section to be put to use so quickly.' She turned to her guests. 'It's barely been open an hour, but where there is need . . .'

The four councillors, three overweight middle-aged men and an overweight middle-aged woman who wore a turquoise-blue toque, edged their way into the reference room, so that now the place felt very crowded.

'Did the gas come down from the ceiling or up from the floor?' Edward thought.

'What are you reading, my boy?' one of the men spoke as if he were in the assembly rooms.

'*Ivanhoe*. It's a set book and—'

'Edward has won a place at Staffley Grammar School. The first boy to do so from his village. He begins in a few weeks' time,' Angela interjected.

'Is your father in business?' the woman in the turquoise toque enquired of Edward.

'No. He's a coal-miner.'

'Oh really? *Really*?' Her response was of such wonderment you might have thought she'd heard something miraculous and yet somehow felt vaguely disappointed with the information, as though this change in the usual order of things boded ill for her in the future.

'Miss Gayle has always helped me. She can find the right book for every subject under the sun. I'm not the first person to be in the reference section today. I had to wait a little while until it was free as all the spaces were taken and—'

'Such a success,' the lady in the hat cut into Edward's accolade. 'We do congratulate you, Miss Gayle, er, without your strenuous efforts most of us are certain this section could never have been added.'

'Yes, yes, yes, yes,' the male members chorused agreement as all four made for an early exit. Perhaps it might have been the light reflected on her face from her hat, but it did seem to Edward that the woman's pallor had taken on a slightly greenish colour, the same colour his Aunty Alice had turned when they had gone out on a Fleetwood fishing boat during a day trip to Blackpool.

When he was sure the visitors had left the building, Edward crept out from the lean-to and gulped in fresh air just as soon as he got into the main building. He was greeted by Angela Gayle as he approached the exit.

'Oh, Edward. You were wonderful. Just wonderful.' She wagged a cautionary finger, 'But I cannot condone tiny lies.'

Edward smiled. He could have mentioned that he'd heard Miss Gayle tell lies that were not so tiny, but accepted the reproof in the false way that it was offered. Miss Gayle began to pack his books up in a brown paper carrier bag, then added two small packages wrapped in greaseproof paper, as though they were an afterthought.

'There's four shrimp and bloater paste sandwiches, a rock cake and an apple. You could have them for your lunch or tea.' She stroked her plait as she spoke. 'Olive always puts out too much for me and it's wicked to waste good food. I don't suppose we shall be seeing so much of you in the future?'

'Why not? Are you going away?' Edward could be brusque – a quality he had inherited from his mother.

'No, no. I mean you will be going to your new school and . . .'

'I'll always come to see you, Miss Gayle. Thank you for the sandwiches.'

Miss Gayle began to gurgle and chuckle, 'Oh, Edward, Edward. You are a tartar.'

'You mean, like Genghis Khan?'

'No. Like – Like – Like my friend Olive.'

CHAPTER FIVE

Once outside the library, Edward's step lightened. The air was fresh and cold but there was some sun visible in a steel-grey sky. His lunch was in the carrier bag and he had fourpence in his pocket; a leisurely tour of the town held greater appeal when there was money to spend.

He paused and scanned the names on the war memorial. It was of interest to him that his mother's father's name was listed among the men who died in the 1914–18 war. Edward offered this homage almost every time he came through the town. His grandparents on both sides of his family were all dead before he was eighteen months old. There was no recollection of them for him and other children were always going to see or spending time with a granny or grandad. This lack of a link with the past often made him feel further displaced. He'd always had a sneaking admiration for baby cuckoos; it wasn't their fault their parents had chosen to plonk them into a nest that didn't really want them.

It was true, he had lots of uncles and aunties; his father came from a family of nine brothers who all met with great regularity and a wall of fraternal secrecy which would have done credit to the Knights Templar. Amongst their offspring there were two girl cousins who Edward loved. His cousin Rona, who was eighteen, married with a child of two and who worked as a bus conductress, lived in a prefab. Sometimes he would take his baths there and occasionally stay overnight. She had taught him to cook, to iron, to sew buttons on coats, as if she had some insight into the future. She would also kiss him firmly on the forehead and leave her lipstick imprint there like some temporary tattoo. His cousin Doreen was three years younger than Edward but loved him to make up stories for her. Her questions indicated an intelligence beyond her years and she would eagerly listen to any of Edward's current enthusiasms. She would save half her sweet ration for him, knowing that his mother only allowed a couple of toffees or one square of chocolate a week at the very most to fall in his direction.

His mother never spoke of her relations except to say they were all gone from her.

'Why should you worry yourself. You've got nine uncles, nine aunties, twenty-nine cousins, all living within five miles of you. Isn't that enough for you to be getting on with?'

There were two cafés in the town and Edward's parents had never visited either of them. As far as he knew, they had never eaten a meal or even drunk a cup of tea in any kind of commercial establishment. His mother would have found the economics of such a venture unappealing and his father would have felt socially uncomfortable.

'We've got a table, chairs, crockery and cutlery – why sit somewhere else to eat and drink when you can sit at home?'

There always seemed to be more prams and push-chairs than people in the British Restaurant and the three women counter assistants always looked depressed and listless. Young children fretted and squawked and played tag between the tables and cups of stewed tea were always getting spilt on to the floor. The place held no joy or interest for Edward. The Rainbow Milk Bar was another matter. The counter was situated at the far end of an oblong room that seemed so much longer than it really was on account of the top halves of the two side walls being covered by mirrors. Shining chrome bar stools were attached to the floor close to the walls and drink rests jutted out from the walls conveniently placed for glasses and elbows. By looking in the mirror facing them, customers could cast interested glances at someone sitting on the opposite side of the room without appearing to look too pushy or forward. Many romances in Batsford had reflection as their source.

Romance in this arena had never interested Edward, nor, for that matter, had the beverages pleased him greatly. You could, of course, order tea, lemonade or a glass of Tizer, but people somehow instigated a peculiar type of snobbery that looked down on such orders. Milk shakes were the order of the day. Flavours included chocolate, banana, orange, lemon and vanilla. Edward had tried all of them and had found the frothy concoctions too sweet and sickly for his teeth. Now even the strong odour of these drinks made his stomach feel queasy and nauseous.

Yet Edward lingered and looked. It was the illuminated giant music box which held his attention. It was called a Wurlitzer and held within its glowing yellow innards no less than sixty records. At the press of a select button, Johnny Ray could rise up from its depths, sail across on to a playing deck and sing at your personal command.

Some people already had radiograms at home. Thirteen year olds like himself even had their own record collections. His mother said they could not afford one and she wouldn't buy anything on the knock, not even an electric cooker and they needed an electric cooker before they had a radiogram. Edward could never quite accept his mother's poverty-pleading. Other families larger than theirs, where only one parent worked, seemed to possess more small luxuries than they did. Only recently his mother had complained about their state of living.

'I don't know what the bloody hell we've won this war for. We're no better off now than when it was going full pelt. Worse in some ways, I'm earning less and you're doing no better.'

'Oh come on now, Esther. We've enough food for our stomachs and lots of people who couldn't see to read or see anything much further than the next lamppost have got glasses,' his father chuckled and added, 'and I've got some new teeth in my mouth now that don't move about as though they had St Vitus' Dance. And if we get sick we can see a doctor or go to the hospital without ending up in debt for months.'

His mother had grunted but had not been consoled. If she had known that some of Edward's meagre pocket money had been spent in the milk bar, she would have felt that she had been purposefully cheated or embezzled in some way. Edward never mentioned anything that veered close to self-indulgence to his mother.

He watched as a girl strolled insolently across the floor. Her face, made expressionless by a heavy mask of pan-stick, moved this way and that as she crushed between her jaws the chewing gum which half-filled her mouth. A tall youth, with sleeked-back black hair that glistened and dripped with Brylcreem, stood by her side and chose the records after she had fed the money into the machine. The two of them ignored the large sign above the jukebox which read NO DANCING and took centre floor to a big band piece from Stan Kenton. As the couple turned, the youth's eyes looked blankly at

Edward as if he were not there with his face close to the window pane. For his part, Edward wondered how anybody with so many pimples and pustules on his face could be so vain.

Further down the road, Edward was happy to dawdle about the entrance to the Royale cinema. If any building could have been more inaptly named then Edward was sure you would have to go a long way to find it. The Royale was the old-age pensioner of Batsford's cinemas and, from the state of its exterior and interior, and from the pleasures it had to offer, its days were numbered.

The Royale had begun life as a hall for a non-conformist religious sect which had faded away from lack of membership. It was now strictly a family affair. Mr Perkins hired the films and manned the operation, his wife, May, sold the tickets at the box office and his two daughters, June and Valerie, alternated with each other as usherettes. Both daughters had half-caste sons eight years of age and it was rumoured that the same American GI had sired both children. True or false, the rumours did not seem to give too much stress to the girls or their parents. This was a close-knit family that went to the pictures together and stayed together.

Everyone in and around Batsford referred to the Royale as the Umbrella. Anyone not of local origin could hardly have fathomed the reason for such an odd nomenclature. The lack of ventilation in the long, low-ceilinged hall always led to profuse condensation on the walls and ceilings of the building so that by the end of a long programme (and in terms of value for money, the programmes were long) the audience would feel gentle spots of warm water drip on their heads and splash on to the back of their necks. Such natural happenings had on occasion ruined the orgasms of courting couples sitting in the back row of the cinema,

47

but, as Mr Perkins had rightly stated, 'If they had come here to look at the pictures, then they'd have nothing to complain about.'

Cowboy films seemed to fill most of the week's agenda. By now Edward knew that crooks in these films usually had pencil-thin moustaches. Groups of riders would rush this way and that and, if you kept a watchful eye on the screen, you would see that the riders might often pass through the same terrain more than once, pause at the same clump of pine trees and even sit on the same, convenient-looking boulders. He didn't feel that three B feature films were any better value than one A.

Then, like some young, unsuspecting prospector, he sighted gold. It was there staring him right in the face; the Royale Sunday Special. Fourpenny roll-up, for one day only, commencing at two pm. A continuous performance until ten-thirty pm. The trio of films was entitled *Song and Dance*. There was *Meet Me In Saint Louis* with Margaret O'Brien and Judy Garland. Margaret was the only child star Edward could stomach as she was often sad, and nowadays Judy Garland didn't have to be accompanied by Micky Rooney. There was *State Fair* with Jeanne Craine and a black and white film starring Ann Sothern called *Congo Maisie*. From the stills outside, Edward knew all these films could offer him temporary rapture. The fourpence in his pocket took on greater import and Miss Gayle's bloater paste sandwiches now held all the appeal of sockeye salmon.

'Why aren't you in school?' Edward felt a firm hand grasp his shoulder from behind, in unison with this threatening question.

'Er. What? Pardon?'

Edward's tremulous response brought out bubbles of

48

laughter from the person standing behind him. He
turned to find Lawrence looking down at him, his
shoulders hunched with laughter, his face creased with
smiles.

'It's not that funny,' Edward snapped. 'And what
about yourself?'

'I was only joking, Eddie. You can take a joke, can't
you?'

'I suppose so.' Lawrence could always charm people
even when he didn't mean to. 'I don't have to go back
anymore. Start at my new school in a few days.'

'I'm not going back either.'

'But there's another six or seven weeks before Christmas. You'll have the truant officer coming around.'

Lawrence shrugged.

'Proctor will be lucky if he sees me for five days let
along five weeks. Our mam will give me absence notes.
Anyway, I can help out at home. Our dad's not well. It's
his chest. He's coughing like a steam engine and the
doctor says he has to leave the pit bottom and work on
the back.'

'It will be better for his health.'

'It might be better for his health but it won't do his
pocket any good, Edward. Our mam says she doesn't
know how she's going to manage. She's having another
one early next year. I hope it's not a girl. Two sisters are
enough for me.'

Lawrence had taken Edward's books from his carrier
bag, glanced at them admiringly and replaced them
carefully.

'Good. Very good, Eddie,' he muttered and then, as if
to bring talk to ground that was more familiar to him,
'it's lovely weather for early November. What a change
from a few days back. Are you getting a bus back to the
village?'

'Yes. Erm. I mean, no. No. I'm walking. I want to save the fare.'

'I'm going back over the stiles. We're short of food for our rabbits and they've just cropped a field of cabbages that way. There'll be enough there to keep them happy for a week or more.'

'How many have you got?'

'Twenty-two. Or twenty-four. It's hard to count all the small ones. Oh, tell your mam she can have a buck for two bob if she wants one. My dad will skin it for her.'

They left the town together and talked little but Edward felt oddly content this way in Lawrence's company.

'He hasn't got a bad thought in his head,' Edward's father had said of Lawrence's father and Edward now realised this was true of the son too.

As they passed the first hedgerows and negotiated the first stile, Edward noted Lawrence's easy gracefulness as he leap-frogged over the post, arms straight and firm, long legs splayed out wide, landing on the other side as though everyone could pass such an obstacle with such sureness. Edward pitched forward but managed to stay on his feet thanks to Lawrence, who rushed to support him as he stumbled. A flock of birds hurtled across the sky.

'They're late leaving. Should have left us a good three weeks ago. I expect this bit of mild weather has fooled them.'

'Mmm.' Eddie agreed with Lawrence's observation. Lawrence knew all about such things. He knew where the first hazelnuts would ripen in the coppice wood, where to find the best watercress in the streams that ran from the canal to the meadows, which blackberries would be easy picking on the railway banks, the largest bilberry patches on the heath and –

'He's like my father,' Edward thought. 'He loves this place.'

Now Edward noticed that Lawrence was carrying his bag for him. He couldn't remember passing it to him. He wanted to look at Lawrence's face but felt unaccountably shy, as though Lawrence had suddenly turned into a grown-up.

'The field's up there, on the hill, just the other side of the pill-box.' Edward's gaze followed the outstretched arm and index finger as Lawrence pointed out his destination. 'They cropped the cabbages the day before yesterday so there should be plenty of pickings left. It doesn't look like it but that hillock is the highest point round here for miles.'

'That's why the pill-box is there. It was for observation during the war,' Edward observed.

'Funny. I always thought it was for machine guns when I was a little kid. All set to mow down the Germans when they landed. But there was no reason for them to land here, was there? I suppose you're right, Eddie. From there they could keep an eye on things and with field glasses they could see for maybe fifteen miles or more.'

Like most war infants, the memories of the time were indelibly imprinted in their minds. In case they might forget, there were any number of testaments still standing to act as reminder. Two bomb craters, now water-filled, stagnated not far from their homes. Pathetic-looking deserted air-raid shelters studded back gardens and some had been moved piece by piece to serve a more utilitarian purpose on allotments as crude, evil-smelling toilets. Many houses still maintained black-out curtains as privacy seemed more important than light and people wished for a more individual and less collective existence. Ration books remained omnipresent and motor cars were scarce to the region. Bread and milk were still delivered by horse and cart, people queued in orderly fashion for food, transport or entertainment and men still wore their shiny, ill-fitting demob suits on Sundays.

'We are scavengers, Eddie,' Lawrence remarked as he sought out the choicest leaves and stalks, 'Like crows or vultures,' he added laughingly.

'No. Gleaners. We're like pigeons or doves. It's not grass we're picking at, is it?' Edward stretched and placed a handful of greens into the hessian sack that Lawrence held out for him. 'Nearly full,' he muttered, regretting that the task was almost over.

Working side by side with Lawrence brought him sharply into Edward's focus. There was thick, coarse, black hair badly cropped so tufts stuck in odd directions on his head and formed points of rebellion to any comb. Dark brown eyes with heavy, crescented eyebrows that all but met at the bridge of his nose. His complexion was sallow but the outdoor life had given it a slightly golden glow. Like his body, his face was long and thin, the nose aquiline, the lips full. On the jaw and above the upper lip, Edward could see dark shadows of hair growth. Fine dark hairs also adorned the backs of the arms. The face in repose seemed sad or sullen even, but when Lawrence smiled it was slow and gentle. The missing tooth lent an unconscious charm to all of this. And now, at this point in time, Edward saw that Lawrence, who he had never regarded in such a light before, was beautiful.

'That's it, then.' Lawrence looked with satisfaction into the sack. Edward held the edges together as he twined string about the top. Their arms touched. Edward felt strangely aroused by this slight physical contact, whilst Lawrence seemed unaware of it and continued to seal the sack's contents, tying a swift, secure knot with the adept air of a natural artisan. Edward desperately wished to delay their departure from the spot and he knew why he wanted to delay it. As a last resort, he blurted out in a foolish manner, experiencing embarrassment on hearing his own words, 'I wonder if there are any owls in the pill-box. I have missed seeing our pair.'

'There'll be none there, Edward,' Lawrence spoke as he would have done to a child, gently correcting a careless observation. 'There's nothing for them to feed on around here. No voles or mice. They need a good feeding area. Anyway, they wouldn't get in and out through those small peep-holes very easily.'

He hauled the bag over his shoulder but saw that Edward stood still and was making no effort to move. Edward seemed to be looking at his throat which was exposed as the three top buttons of his checked shirt were left undone. He flicked at his chest and neck.

'I haven't got a creepy-crawly on me, have I? It's not a wasp, is it?'

Edward reached forward and touched the fine hairs at the top of Lawrence's chest.

'When did these come?' he murmured.

'Not overnight, but I reckon I could look like an ape before I'm twenty-one.'

Edward did not remove his hand, but stroked the hair, pulling it gently with his fingertips. Lawrence moved closer to him, the sack still held over his shoulders. Edward cast his eyes downwards and saw the bulge in the trousers that stood so near to him. He placed his hand there. He'd never touched a cock apart from his own before and it made him feel secretive and excited. Lawrence, too, had become infected with this tension. He remained still but managed to speak in a low, confidential tone.

'Perhaps we should look inside the pill-box anyway before we go.'

The inside of the building smelled damp and dark and, with its octagonal-shaped walls and small steps leading up to the observations slots in each side, the place still held some sense of secret plots and confidential knowledge. Beams of light from the observation holes crisscrossed the gloom and specks of dust danced about in the rays as if they were under the scrutiny of a powerful microscope. If magic could really be performed, and if spells could be cast, then this was surely a place for them.

Lawrence walked about studying the floor space before he could declare it too wet to sit down anywhere. Edward called out to him.

'Over here. Come over here, Lawrence.' Edward stood on the lowest of one of the steps with his back against the wall. Whatever was about to take place, he knew it was he who would be orchestrating it. 'We are about the same height now.' He stroked the bulge in Lawrence's trousers and felt the outline of the balls beneath the erection.

The rabbit fodder fell to the floor as Lawrence unclipped Edward's braces suddenly, as if in great haste, almost like someone in a great state on discovering food. With his clothing about his ankles, Edward unbuttoned Lawrence and then took hold of him and, with gentle, confidential whispers, he placed the dick snugly below his own testicles and closed his thighs firmly about it.

'There. There,' was all he said as he placed his arms around Lawrence's neck and urged him forward.

'Oh, it's lovely, lovely, Eddie,' Lawrence gasped as he rubbed to and fro, either hand clasping firmly each of Edward's buttocks.

Edward stroked the back of Lawrence's neck and

could feel the skin of his face against his own. A slight movement to the side by either of them and their lips would have touched. Edward wished for this but made no moves to bring it about. He was sure that this would prove iconoclastic; any number of boys had tossed off together but kissing another boy would be a taboo with the most terrible interpretation put on it. Even in this, that was happening now, the sharing of sexual pleasure went beyond all the limits of his experience. You could indulge in solitary sexual play, you could enjoy it in parallel with someone, but this . . . Lawrence had taken a firmer clutch on his buttocks, his thrusting became more insistent, more rapid, more rhythmical, his breathing heavier and louder as his excitement mounted.

'Oh. Oh. Eddie. I'm going to come. I'm going to—'

'Go on . . . Go on . . . Go on, Lawrence. Come,' Edward commanded.

As Lawrence began to call out, Edward felt the body crashing against him judder in spasms and paroxysms, the wide frame seemed to shake before it became calm and still after expelling its sticky liquid in three or four spurts. Although he had been merely a recipient, Edward felt a strange sense of power and experienced no trace of shame but merely searched his pockets for his handkerchief in order to clean up what Lawrence had so urgently left between his legs.

Lawrence placed a friendly hand on Edward's shoulder as they walked briskly through the fields and meadows, only removing it when they reached the roughly tarmacked lane on the edge of the village which spelt out a parting of their ways.

'You know, Eddie . . . You know, if you were a girl, I'd take you to the pictures.'

With this innocent observation, Lawrence quickly dispelled any ideas that Edward had begun to foster in terms of a romantic alliance. Edward surprised himself by his cleverness at veiling any kind of disappointment.

'I always sit in the balcony, Lawrence, and I like an ice cream in the interval.' He drew Lawrence's attention to his clothing. 'Fasten yourself up. You've left two fly hole buttons undone.'

In this way he had gently let Lawrence know that pretending that absolutely nothing had happened between them was a form of lying that he could not comply with. They both parted from one another deep in the knowledge that a climax had been reached in more ways than one. Their goodbyes were friendly and respectful.

As Edward munched his way through Olive Goodman's paste sandwiches and bit into her aptly described rock cake, the present and immediate future looked bright and pleasant. He had no intention of ever setting eyes on that prison they had called a school ever again. He began his new school after the half term break was over, and he had the pictures to look forward to on Sunday. And, before that day, there was Bonfire Night.

Sunday held an extra appeal as it was one of the Sundays on which he had the house to himself. These Sundays, one in every month, Edward referred to as his parents' *mystery days*. Ever since he could remember anything, his mother had put on her best hat and coat and left the house at nine on every fourth Sunday morning, not returning until after seven at night. In the past three years, his father had accompanied her, leaving Edward alone. He had never minded being left behind. He had minded not knowing where they were going or what the reason for it was.

'If it's not important, then why can't you tell me?'

'Ask no questions and you'll meet no lies,' said his mother. 'We need a rest from you.'

'I don't want to come with you. I just want to know where you go.'

'Picking mushrooms.'

'I'd like to see you pick mushrooms in those gloves and high-heeled shoes.'

'Tell him to stop his questions,' his mother told his father. 'Anybody would bloody well think that we're war criminals.'

'That's enough Edward,' his father said gently. 'There's an end to your prying.'

'If our Edward were a cat,' his mother pronounced. 'He'd be bloody well dead.'

Edward no longer asked about their sortie. He accepted it in the same way as he accepted the noise of their lovemaking which he had heard through the paper-thin walls. It was something parents did that you didn't mention or enquire of.

As soon as he heard the click of the latch on the back gate, Edward switched on the electric kettle. He checked that the coal buckets on the hearth were full, saw that the sugar, bowl, tea cup and saucer were arranged on the table. He watched from the window as his father removed his heavy, steel-capped working boots and left them just inside the back kitchen door. As his father entered, pit-grimed and red-eyed, he took his pit bag from him and hung it behind the bogey-hole door. His father settled himself wearily near the table and sighed in a pleased sort of fatigue.

'Well, our Edward. That's another day over. Has it been fair all day?'

Once, Edward had mocked his mother, 'You can only talk about the weather to my dad.'

She had delivered a sharp, swift slap to the back of his head.

'Don't tell me what I should say to your father. If you had been underground all day with not an ounce of sunlight, *you* might like to know what it had been like above in the fresh air.'

'It's been fine,' he told him now. 'Fine all day. Your tea's ready. Shall I pour it?'

'Let it stand a bit, Edward. I like to taste the tea, otherwise it's like drinking maid's water.'

'I've got you a new Zane Grey western from the library. Do you want me to read a bit out to you before mam comes back?'

His father sipped some tea.

'Very nice. A very nice brew, Edward. Just what the doctor ordered. You must have got from school to the library and back here again in double quick time,' he observed unaccusingly.

Edward ignored his father's insight with regard to how he had spent his day.

'I suppose you'd rather read the book yourself.'

'Yes. I think I can manage it. I'll put a little pencil mark under any words I'm not sure of and check them out with you later. I'll get the gist of what's happening and we can rub the pencil marks out later.'

Edward had realised his father was illiterate when he noticed that he sometimes confused one division with another as he checked his football results. In moments when his mother was not present, he had taught his father phonics and then made out lists of key words for him to memorise every day. Words like *because* and *said* which defied the logic of sound and word-building. His mother had feigned unawareness of this activity and now expressed no surprise when her husband browsed through the paper without referring to her. She expressed no resentment or jealousy that her son and her husband were good friends. Her own territory was unassailable.

In turn, Edward's father had taught him to play whist and crib, as well as how to study the form of racehorses. On local history he would give Edward a pageant of working lives that went back two or three generations; who rode the first bicycle, how many men were killed in pit disasters, bare-knuckle fist fights, dog-fights, the big strike, how someone had been hanged at Stafford jail for murdering his wife and cutting her up into bits and pieces, and how it was they knew it was her when a stray dog unearthed her left leg which had a big scald mark near the thigh bone.

'So you see, if she hadn't scalded herself badly when she was fifteen, he would never have faced the drop.'

Edward's father had always talked to him as though he were an adult, and for this Edward was grateful.

Two hours later, Edward performed a similar ritual for his mother but she drank her tea without commenting on it and showed scant interest in his new books or the new reference library which smelt of a creosote gas chamber. She seemed to spring to life, however, when Edward mentioned the rabbit.

'Why didn't you tell me when I got in? You forgot? You *forgot*? You know full well your father loves a bit of rabbit stew.' She had roused herself and put on her coat. 'And they might all be gone by the time I get down there.'

'Lawrence said he'd save you one,' Edward responded sullenly.

She paused at the door, knowing that she had been harsh but also knowing that apology of any kind was not part of her relationship with her son. She sought to make amends in a practical way.

'Try your pullover on. I've finished it.' She lit a cigarette. 'It's the front room. Go on. Put on all your uniform. Let's see what you are going to look like for your new school.'

'Ah. Ah well. I don't know, our Eddie,' his father exclaimed as Edward appeared before them, entering from the front as though he were an actor moving from the wings to the footlights. Edward admiringly viewed his reflection in the sideboard mirror.

'It's maroon and gold,' he breathed.

'No. It's scarlet,' his mother corrected. 'You're a scarlet boy. You'll stick out like a sore thumb in this village.'

Edward frowned. He ought to have been used to her lack of enthusiasm for anything that seemed important to him, yet he often winced inwardly. He did not reveal any injury but said, 'That's what I'll be then. A scarlet boy.'

'I'm off to get this rabbit.' She ignored Edward and addressed his father. 'He's a brazen little bugger. Brazen.'

'The apple don't fall far from the tree, Esther,' his father called out to her as Edward stood looking at himself in the mirror. It was still a few days to Bonfire Night but in some ways Edward felt that the fireworks had already started. He smiled and adjusted his tie.

CHAPTER SIX

By the springtime of the following year, Edward's mother's sharp observation seemed some distance from present reality. He did not *stick out like a sore thumb* in his own village, largely because he was rarely seen there. And when he was there, he felt as if he were a visitor, not a resident.

In some ways, Edward's relationship with his mother had now come to resemble the foreign politics of the day. A cold war existed between them. There were resentments, mutterings, isolation from one another and an obdurate refusal by both to recognise the solidity of each other's way of life.

His father had remained neutral, but Edward saw much more of him now than at any other time he could recall. The journey to and from school each day served to remind him how little he had travelled and how intensely parochial his existence had been. He had seen the sea twice, once at Rhyl and once at Blackpool. These excursions had been one-day coach trips for children from his father's working men's club. The bus rides had been noisy and long, so that only a few hours were available on the beach, and then most of the children had played football. Edward had remained alone most of the time, writing his name in the sand with the heel of his shoe and watching the small breakers erase it almost as soon as it was done.

His scholarship provided him with a journey every day which was considerably shorter but infinitely more variable in human terms and mode of transport. By any standards, it was a long trip and most boys would have found it exhausting. For Edward, his bus and train passes acted as passports of liberation from a ghetto as real to him as anywhere in an Eastern European country.

The early morning belonged to him and his father and the loving routine and ritual of their dawn preparations never varied.

'Eddie. Eddie. Come on. Time to get up. It's ten to five. Ssh. Don't wake your mam. There's some tea and toast on the table. See that you eat all the toast. You shouldn't leave the house on an empty stomach.' He placed Edward's chair close to the fire and here, in his striped pyjamas, Edward munched on his toast, drank his sweet tea and contemplated the day ahead. The atmosphere of affectionate care that his father engendered during this time was precious to him. 'I'll give your shoes another brushing. It's no good just putting polish on without some elbow grease. There. Now there's plenty of hot water in the kettle for you to wash. See that you don't leave a tide-mark around your neck and soak the flannel and wipe under your arms. Always remember to clean under your arms, now. You don't want to be like Ralph Stratton, do you?'

'Who is Ralph Stratton?'

'Works down J's pit. Single. You couldn't meet a nicer bloke. He's as good as they come but he stinks like an otter.'

Before they left, there was always a joint inventory of possessions.

'Got me snap-bag. There's your satchel. Here's me helmet. Put your cap on. All times you're supposed to wear it. Got all the books you need? Here's me lamp and bottle of water. It's Wednesday, have you got your sports things?' And then he would put some coal slack on the fire, glance up towards the clock and say, 'We'd best be off. I hate last minute rushes.'

The first transport of the day that the village could witness was the pit bus, and Edward and his father were always the first to await its arrival at a quarter past six. Edward had complained mildly that perhaps they arrived a little too early and had put a case forward for not having twenty minutes to spare standing about at the stop.

'Now, Edward. What if the bus came a bit early one day. Or what if we learned it had broken down? If it came early, we would still catch it and if we learned it had broken down, we could walk, hell for leather, into Batsford. And I'd still be at the pit on time and you'd catch the train.'

Appearances counted for a great deal at Edward's new school. It was made more than clear that demeanour and behaviour outside school were probably more important than within it. 'One boy could ruin the good name of the school,' was flung out so often it would be impossible to forget, so that the uniform seemed to mark you out as a paragon, a sort of envoy from Heaven who let lesser mortals on Earth know that privilege was correlated with perfection. Even now, he had come to realise that courtesy and good manners were not necessarily anything to do with social etiquette. His father proved this, the way he greeted people, the way he expressed concern for someone else's distress, the way he would hold off from speaking ill of anyone, his acceptance of people different from himself – all seemed to stem from an innate sense of good manners.

Edward mirrored this pattern in his own behaviour and reaped the rewards it offered. He was well liked at school and within the village. On reflection he felt some small traces of guilt about this because, unlike his father, he was more than capable of insincerity in turning situations to his own advantage by false praise or fake interest.

His fellow passengers on the pit bus, all miners, would not talk a great deal among themselves after their initial greetings. Edward always sat apart from the company on a single seat close to the bus driver. On occasion one of them might make some remark to him.

'You're not following your dad down the pit, then, Eddie?'

'His hands aren't made for humping coal, nor his eyes for darkness,' his father would answer.

'What are you going to do when you leave, Eddie?'

Here again, his father would gently intervene, somehow knowing that Edward could not answer this question. Ambition of any kind had never been a part of his environment.

'He can tap-dance for all I care, as long as he's not down the pit.'

'He won't earn much tap-dancing, Richard.'

'As long as he's content and happy enough, then that's it.' No-one quarrelled with this point of view and one of them would call out to Eddie, 'He's a good man, your father. A good man.'

'I know that,' Edward agreed with the utmost sincerity. He would also like to have said, 'And he's an interesting man. It's not only nasty people who are interesting.' But he nodded and the passengers were assured of the firm bonding between fledgling and cock pheasant in spite of the plumage being reversed.

When the bus absorbed its main body of passengers at Batsford, Edward was expelled from it. He always got the sensation that all the men would begin to talk as soon as he had alighted, just in the same way that pupils talked when teachers left the room. From Batsford town centre, he walked a quarter of a mile to the railway station, which was situated on a branch line which ran all the way from Birmingham right up beyond Trentfield and even past Uttoxeter. In its journey, this steam train traversed the factories and chimneys of the Black Country and passed into the chase and heath land of North Staffordshire in a trip with as many changes in landscape as it had station stops. It rarely belched and snorted for much more than fifteen minutes before grinding to a halt at some small village whose name would not be familiar to anyone who did not live there.

Mr Finch, the sole employee at Batsford Station at this early hour, was a thin, pasty-faced man of thirty who looked closer to fifty. His sour outlook and grudging temperament caused all the other boys to steer well clear of him. Yet, with an admixture of flattery ('this station would go to the dogs without you, Mr Finch') and an excessively pleasant good morning greeting, Edward had managed to inveigle himself into Mr Finch's tiny reservoir of good will. During the cold winter months this had brought him special favours.

'You can sit in the ladies waiting room until the others arrive. There's a fire lit in there and you can get yourself warm. It's not open to those other snipe-nosed little buggers though.'

'Thank you, Mr Finch.' Edward was truly grateful as he had to wait half an hour for his train. The fifteen or so other boys usually arrived five or ten minutes before its departure. At this point Mr Finch would impart some ghastly piece of information.

'The young lad that they took on as a trainee in the signal box is off sick. Been away for over a month now. Mumps. Bad age for him to get mumps. They say his tentacles got to such a size that if he could have walked, he'd have to push them around in front of him with a wheelbarrow.'

'Oh, how terrible for him, Mr Finch.'

'Yes. He won't marry now. If he does, he won't get much out of it. I was never too keen on the lad, myself. Have you had mumps yet?'

Apart from Mr Finch, Edward loved train travel. He did not let the other boys know that this was his very first experience of such a mode of transport and from the very first day he had been enchanted by it. The privacy of the carriages, the noise and rhythm of the moving train, the vista from the windows, the comfort and even the smell of the steam engine as it snorted to a halt, all helped to conjure up the feeling in his head that each new day was an adventure.

His time passed in the waiting room was never misspent. He would chant his Latin declensions and French verbs, read his set English literature books, so he was always two or three chapters ahead of the others, and he would study the continents of the world till he knew where the Orinoco and the Amazon flowed and which spidery blue lines indicated the great water masses of the Mississippi, Nile, Ganges and Yangtze Kiang.

He would always join in with the other boys when they bemoaned the fact that they hadn't completed their homework. This was a small deceit as he had always done it. Apart from algebraic quadratic equations, he never found such duties irksome. Private study, for the most part, was a world of discovery for Edward and he did not resent it.

There were four stops before the train reached Trentfield. The second of these halts held the greatest fascination. Pine Halt had to be one of the smallest railway stations in the world. The wooden sheds that faced each other on either side of the rough platforms made out of disused railway sleepers constituted its entire architecture. There were no houses or thorough-fares visible in its immediate environs and it was easy to wonder what kind of service such a desolate spot required.

A glance towards the skyline revealed huge outcrops of heather and fern. Where this ended the landscape was taken up by pine forest which looked forbidding in its symmetrical uniformity. Somewhere in between the forestation and the heather a cluster of huts made up an RAF barracks which housed a thousand or so inmates. The majority of these were young men between the ages of eighteen and twenty going through their two years' National Service. This peacetime militia seemed to have been placed in an environment which made up for the hostile activities no war could presently offer.

When in a romantic frame of mind, Edward imagined the place to be part of a western film set, but when the weather was cold or bleak he could see that, as far as the young men were concerned, the place resembled a very respectable open prison. If these airmen had parachuted from the sky (very few were ever to go near an aeroplane) then they might have felt a little unlucky if they had landed on their feet near Pine Halt.

When the boys left the train at Trentfield, they walked another mile to the grammar school, which had been founded in the small market town way back in Tudor times in the reign of Henry VIII. None of its present buildings maintained this sense of history and the classrooms and planning dated from somewhere in the mid-1930s. The playground was bordered on one side by a main road and on the other by a churchyard wall which banded neglected graves and the shell of a Tudor church that was beyond renovation.

The three additional classrooms that had been built after the war to absorb a clientele which did not pay school fees, had caused Edward to feel one of his few moments of disappointment. He had not expected to spend most of his day sitting in a prefab Nissen hut. At least he did not have to share a desk with anyone else and he was relieved to find out that he was not positioned directly beneath one of the overhead gas heaters which hung like smelly, glowing meteorites from the ceiling.

Boredom, which had been the chief essence of his former school, rarely entered the day here. Each day saw several changes of subject matter and just in human terms there were a variety of adults on view and some of them were very enthusiastic about what they were paid to teach. Within three months, Edward clawed his way from a b-stream banding into an a and from thereon he maintained a place among the first ten pupils when the fortnightly performance lists were read out. For the first time in his school life, he enjoyed a degree of popularity he had not known before and he received praise, which was welcome to him as much as any new experience.

He had taken his first report home and placed it on the table. His father had taken it up first and spent a great deal of time deciphering the information but eventually smiled very broadly and shook his head in disbelief as though he had won the football pools.

'Well, I don't know. Well I don't know, our Edward. Very good. Very good.'

His mother watched, eagle-eyed, as his father gave him a half-crown. This seemed to prod her interest into what was written on Edward's report. She read it and her face showed neither interest nor elation. Her eyes rested on the right-hand corner of the paper which indicated Edward's position in class. She peered over the report sheet as she held it between her thumb and forefinger.

'You came second, then?'

'Yes. You can see I did.'

'Oh. Some boy beat you, then.'

Later his father had tried to assuage Edward's wounds.

'She doesn't mean it, Eddie. It's just her way. I'm sure she's as pleased as punch when the cards are down.'

'The only card game she ever played was snap.'

'Now, Eddie. I won't have you running your mother down. You wouldn't find a better woman if you searched Batsford for ten years.' Edward had not responded further.

'If I had been evacuated during the war,' he thought, 'I might have found a lady that was sweet and kind, who wore scent all the time and would kiss me on the forehead or the cheek now and again and who talked more and listened more and –'

Her reservations towards Edward's present schooling had festered into downright resentment. This was fed by the correctness of her prediction that it would demand extra expense from the home. As well as white shirts and grey stockings, sports gear had to be paid for: shorts, house team shirts and white cricket flannels. Then there were trips to the theatre in Stratford-on-Avon to fund. Edward felt grim and despondent each time he was required to ask for something. At one time, he had felt the deepest shame.

'I have to have some underpants. Everyone else has them.'

'Have to? *Have* to? Your father has never worn such things in his life. What do you think your shirt-tail is for? Pull it up between your legs.'

69

'Some of the boys have noticed in the changing room. It's embarrassing.'

'I'll get you a pair from the market.'

'I'll need three pairs. I need to change them. I can't wear the same underpants for a week.'

'I don't see why not if you wipe your bottom carefully. It's the same with your shirts. If you looked after yourself, two would last the week with no effort. It's all money with you. You would think we were made of it.'

Eddie thought no such thing, yet he found it hard to understand why the family's economic circumstances were as dire as his mother suggested. Both his parents worked, there were only three mouths to feed and the rent of their house was seven and sixpence – it wasn't worth a penny more. Small luxuries which other less wealthy households had taken on were not indulged in. There was no radiogram, walls were still distempered not papered, a tablecloth only appeared on the table on Sundays and there was no heating whatsoever apart from the one coal fire in the living room. His mother would never consider any purchase unless she could pay for it in cash.

'Knock? *Knock?!* Hello, Mrs Warrington. Take what you want today and pay it off for the next six months. No thanks. I'll pay for what I can afford. Nothing more. I want to be owing to no-one.'

Matters reached a crucial point on the second Saturday of the Easter term. It was twenty past six in the evening. His father was not at home and Edward wondered how he was to impart his news to his mother. Perhaps it would be best to tell her what he had done just before *The Archers* started. This was a new serial to which his mother had become addicted. Edward did not share her passion for the programme as it seemed to him that she was far more interested in the lives of the players in this family saga than she was in his. The introductory music began to play.

'I've given up my job.' Edward tried to sound non-chalant. The music had stopped and the voice was saying, 'An everyday story of—' before the sentence was slaughtered in mid-air by the click of the switch.

'You've done what?'

'I'm not delivering bread and cakes anymore. I told them at the bakery after the round was finished. They were quite understanding about it.'

'Oh, were they now? Well, I'm not. What's the matter with you? Have you lost a leg or an arm or something?'

'People from my school have seen me.'

As he spoke, Edward recalled his sense of shame as he had driven the village cob horse and cart through Batsford. He had brought the animal to a pause at a side street before entering the main road which led to the bakery. From the side of his cab he saw the three boys in scarlet coats. One was pointing a finger towards him. He heard his name. He did not respond but leaned back deep into the recess of the cab. Only his hands on the reins were now visible and no-one could recognise a pair of hands. If he were quick he could escape, deny all knowledge of his present occupation.

With a small jerk of the reins he had urged the cob forward. The horse responded as though Satan were whispering something in his ear. There was not one loud fart, but three in succession. The animal's flanks twitched in anticipation before the arse opened and expelled great dollops of manure on to the road in steady plops.

'Save it for your rhubarb, Eddie,' he heard one voice call out. Still he did not acknowledge their presence or declare his identity. By the time he had unsaddled the horse at the depot, his sense of humiliation was so great, he felt as deeply disgraced as if he himself had been caught shitting in the middle of the high road. The incident seemed closer to a nightmare than reality.

His present state of dejection brought no sympathy from his mother.

'So what? What's that got to do with giving up your Saturday job? People see me working at the market. What's wrong with honest labour?'

'Do you think I want everyone at school to know I do a bread round? Can't you understand it's not the sort of thing boys at our school should do. It's like eating chips out of the paper in the street or not wearing a tie.'

'How the hell are you *supposed* to eat chips? Stuff them in your ears? And what's a tie got to do with anything? Hitler was never without one, so it can't always be a recommendation.'

Edward let his head drop forward so that his chin rested on his chest. It was no use saying any more, although there was a bit more that he could say, a lot more that he felt ashamed and angry about. He was given no time to lick wounds real or imaginary. His mother's anger surpassed his.

'I'm sick to the back teeth of your la-di-da ways. We're not good enough for you, are we? Neither me nor your dad. We're not the pedigree you wanted, are we? Well, this is your home until you are old enough to leave it and our ways are good enough for us and while you are here they can be bloody good enough for you. I can't speak for you finding something wrong with what I have to say and no I won't stop swearing and you can still use newspaper to wipe your arse on and Lifebuoy soap to wash your hands and face with and if your father wants to belch or fart he can do it whenever he likes in this house. You don't pay the rent or provide the food. It's high time you were laying money on the table, not books.'

'I don't see what all that has to do with me giving up my job,' Edward ventured his opinion quietly.

'Oh don't you, now? Mr Hoity Toity doesn't know. I work.' She prodded her own chest as she spoke. 'Your dad goes into work whether or not he's sick or well. You'd have him go down that pit if he was on his last legs.'

'No, I wouldn't,' Edward remonstrated in the face of this unfairness.

'I'll see to it your father gives you no more pocket money – not a penny – and nothing for *extras* as your precious school calls them. And what's more . . .'

Edward couldn't cope with any more ire and bile and had moved from his seat on his way to the comforting isolation of his bedroom.

'And what is more . . . you are *leaving* that school.'

Edward stopped in his tracks as though an arrow had pierced him between the shoulder blades. He turned round and faced her.

'What do you mean?' he asked, unable to camouflage the fact that he had been seriously wounded.

'I mean what I say. Unless you get another job by next Saturday, you will leave that school when you are fifteen and go to work just like everybody else in this village. You're able-bodied. There's nothing to stop you earning your keep.'

'I won't be able to take my school certificate and . . .' Edward could not keep the mortified tone from his voice.

'Don't talk to me,' she cut in on his appeal.

Edward left the room and made his way upstairs. He took his books from his satchel. He had completed his French and Latin translation exercises and proved a theorem. There was only *Palgrave's Golden Treasury of Verse* to take his mind off the full horrors of what had just gone before. If he did have to leave school at fifteen – and his mother called the tune as far as most things went between her and his father – then what in God's name would he do? The colliery was out of the question. And he knew he couldn't work on a grinder at the edge and tool works like Lawrence did. He suddenly saw himself as a junior sales boy in a furniture shop or at a large tailors like Burtons or Dunns. He looked white-faced, dutiful and bored with servitude. No. He couldn't do that. Well . . . He could . . .

He leafed through his *Palgrave's Golden Treasury* and the poems transported him safely from the shop floor. He knew he had a chance of taking one of the three recitation prizes on offer this term. Mrs Daventry, the wife of Major Daventry, his headmaster, was the judge of the competition this year and, although he only saw her for half an hour each week for singing and music appreciation, he had never failed to compliment her on her rendering of *Drink to Me Only* or *The Trout*.

The poem he chose to memorise suited his present state of mind and speaking the words out loud he somehow managed to find a trace of defiance in its meaning and resonances. He spoke the words to an audience unknown to him. He spoke out, not in self-pity but in wild audacity.

'*The Changeling* by Charlotte Mew. *Toll me no bell, dear Father. Dear mother, waste no sighs . . .*'

He really did understand this feeling of non-belonging, this feeling of not being part of what you have been born into. Perhaps, if he had been evacuated during the war, he might have been looked after by a lady who wanted to be a mother.

'Was I a good baby, Mam? Did you breastfeed me?'

'Babies are babies. They are not good or bad. You were the same as any other. I saw to one end of you with Cow and Gate Powder from a tin and warm water, and your father saw to the other end most of the time.'

'So who held me?'

'The cot did.'

It was one of the longest poems. No-one else would choose it. It could have been written for him. He spoke it out and each time his tone increased in decibel.

'Toll no bell for me, dear Father.

Dear Mother, waste no sighs—'

'Don't worry. We bloody won't!' she bawled out her interruption from the bottom of the stairs.

Edward only paused in his show, like any true artiste, and then completed his ninth rendering in a voice more suitable for an open-air auditorium than a bedroom.

He thought of people who had overcome enormous adversity in order to survive, men like Livingstone, Stanley and Montgomery Clift and women like Florence Nightingale, Odette and Scarlet O'Hara.

'I'll get a job,' he thought. 'I won't be beaten through the ground by her. I'll make her want to say my name over and over and over again. Then, when I'm ready, I'll leave here for good. And I'll have a place of my own. Yet I don't know anybody here who lives on their own, apart from old widows and they've always got sons and daughters and grandchildren calling round. I'll never be married. Never. Do men ever live with other men? Angela Gayle lives with Olive Goodman . . . I have to get a job by next Saturday.'

CHAPTER SEVEN

'There's a lot of people will be upset. At least it wasn't some stupid blabbermouth who sold him down the river this time.' Eddie's mother adjusted her hat as she spoke to his father's reflection in the mirror. 'What fine did he get this time?'

'It was a case of third fine unlucky, Esther. Fifteen pounds.'

'Good God! It's a month's wages down the drain. He doesn't deserve that. He doesn't deserve to be in court at all. What's the difference between putting a bit of money on a horse or a football? If you can afford to go to the racetrack every week, you can bet on a horse. If you can't then you pay a bloody fine for being that much poorer. Bloody silly law. It's only made to be broken.'

'The magistrate said if he comes up again, he's considering sending him to prison for a month.'

'Stupid old bugger. Where did they find him, I wonder? Is my lipstick alright?'

'Just right. He's paid out everybody's winnings. Says he can't collect any bets next week. Says he daren't. Bobby Higton's not going to be too popular for the few months ahead. Now, if you're ready, Esther, we ought to be making off if we're going to catch that bus. Have you got everything?'

'In my bag.' She turned to Edward before leaving. 'You know where the sandwiches are and I've left some cake. You can make some tea if you like. And don't go sniffing and rummaging all about this house the moment we've gone through that door. I'll know if you have. And don't sulk.'

'Has Mr Starsbrook got into trouble, then?' Edward asked knowingly.

'Your ears would latch on the Morse code from Russia, they're so tuned in.'

His father nodded, and sighed, 'Do as your mother says and don't get your nose into every drawer and cupboard you can find. Cheerio, then, lad.'

Edward smiled, pleasantly excited, as he watched his parents leave by the back gate. It was one of their mystery Sundays and he thanked all the lucky stars in the universe that today was such a day and hoped there would be many more like them. He put on the clean white shirt which had been put by for school on Monday, adjusted his school tie properly, put on his blazer and brushed the shoulders, saw that his shoes were clean and checked the clock. It was a quarter to ten in the morning.

Anyone seeing Edward walking purposefully down his street looking so much the epitome of a decent middle-class boy of decent middle-class parents joyfully making his way to worship at a nearby church, or perhaps even to form part of a Church of England choir, would have felt that all was right with the world and that appearance spoke the truth.

Mr Starsbrook's bungalow was one of the few owner-occupied residences in the village. Its architecture was so unique that when strangers visited, they would stop outside the house and stare in wonderment at the arresting edifice. It had sizeable gardens both front and back. It was painted in brown and yellow and under-neath the windows the letters GWR were written. Mr

Starsbrook was an enterprising man. The plot of land had cost him thirty pounds and the long railway carriage which made up his home he had purchased for twenty pounds. His house was not only the most original dwelling in the village, it was the most spacious. It was viewed by most people with admiration rather than disrespect.

On her knees in the front garden, Bridget Casey plunged young cabbage shoots into the earth with ritualistic ferocity, each plant securely delivered, each hole filled. Mr Starsbrook's wife had left the village for good shortly after the war was over. It was rumoured that she had gone to join a GI in the United States of America but no-one had ever validated this.

'I don't think Mrs Starsbrook has gone off with anybody,' his mother had ventured her opinion flatly as though she had no feelings against errant wives. 'I think she just went off him.'

'Is that a reason for leaving a husband?' Edward had asked.

'How would you like to share a bed with someone who you didn't want to touch, let alone anything else? It's a sad thing all round when that happens. Pointing the big finger is a hypocritical game.'

As Edward walked along the garden path, Bridget remained unaware of his presence. Two years after his wife had left him, Mr Starsbrook had gone to London for three days and brought back his deaf and dumb housekeeper with him. She had remained with him ever since and people readily admitted that she seemed happy enough. Others hinted that she shared his bed, but Edward's mother thought it no concern of theirs whether she did or not.

'She's better off with him than being a dogsbody to three or four cantankerous priests. I'm sure George

Starsbrook wouldn't force her to do anything she didn't want to do.'

Most people had now begun to grow a few flowers if they were fortunate enough to have front gardens, but Edward's stroll up the garden path took him past onion sets, runner beans, rows of carrots and potatoes and a patch of radishes and lettuce which almost met the asbestos-sheeted front porch. As he approached, he saw that his short journey had been noted from one of the carriage windows.

'Morning, lad. What can I do for you?' Mr Starsbrook began to search his pocket for a coin. 'Are you collecting for somebody who's passed over or is it one of the churches wants something again? Are you Esther Warrington's son?'

'Yes.' Worst luck, Edward thought, as he nodded and spoke simultaneously. 'There's something I'd like to discuss with you, Mr Starsbrook.'

'Oh? Fire away, then, lad.'

'It's private.'

'Your dad's alright, isn't he? Not been injured or had an accident at the pit or anything like that?'

Edward shook his head then, with a single sweeping arm gesture, Mr Starsbrook invited him in.

'Sit yourself down, lad. I'm just going to put a tie on. I like to wear a tie on Sunday. You see this shirt?' Mr Starsbrook fingered the pale pink material of the garment he was wearing. 'It's nylon. Latest thing, nylon. Called sharkskin. You can't beat a nylon shirt; washes and dries quicker than two shakes of a donkey's tail and always looks smart.'

'It might look smart,' thought Edward, 'but it makes you smell like rancid butter.' Edward caught a whiff of the characteristic odour as Mr Starsbrook passed by him on his way into the next compartment. In spite of knowing that Mr Starsbrook's house was just as firmly secured in the village as anyone else's, Edward still imagined a slight sense of movement, a gentle rocking motion. From the window he half expected to see Bridget Casey and the cabbage plants pass from view and felt some reassurance from her continued presence outside. A message frosted on to the window-pane read: NO SMOKING.

Mr Starsbrook returned wearing a huge tie which had a horse's head painted on it. The main decorative colours were orange, brown, red and green and the horse itself looked cross-eyed. With his red braces, Mr Starsbrook lived up to his usual reputation of being a colourfully dressed man. He was of average height but possessed very broad shoulders and long, ape-like arms which hung at his sides in an awkward way. To compensate for his loss of hair on top of his massive head, he had grown thick, dark, furry sideboard hair which extended right down to his neck. His eyes were of a friendly expression and were very light in colour, his complexion was healthy, and his teeth, like those of most men in the village of his age, were false and ill-fitting.

Edward let him settle himself into the loom chair before making out his case.

'My mother told me about your sad news, Mr Starsbrook. She thinks it's very unfair. The whole village does.'

'That's very kind of her, Edward. A good woman, your mother. Always was.'

'She's very worried for you. She wonders how you're going to manage. The comics and magazines won't bring in enough, will they? At least, she doesn't think they will. She says you are busy at the market but all the money is in pence. I mean, your market work is more of a service than a business, isn't it?'

Mr Starsbrook patted some invisible hair on top of his head into place, blinked his pale blue eyes and stared pensively and unseeingly somewhere above Edward's head. The full import of the recent court's decision entered his large frame for the first time. Things looked bad. He wouldn't starve because Bridget grew enough vegetables to feed four people, but after a pint of beer, cigarettes, a bit of new clothing, there'd be no money left over. He could put in another day at the market but an extra day wouldn't keep Bridget in housekeeping money let alone pocket money. He had a fondness for the woman and he was not a mean man. He only made a penny a purchase on the exchange and sale of second-hand comics and magazines. He glanced over at a great pile of them in the far corner of the long, narrow room and sighed deeply so that his head rose and fell on his shoulders.

'Would you like some comics, Edward? There's *The Wizard, Hotspur, Dandy, Beano, Film Fun*. Your mother might like a few *Silver Star Weeklies*.' His tone was kindly but disconsolate.

'She doesn't read much and I only like books.'

'Oh. I'm sorry. I can't offer you anything then.'

'You can, Mr Starsbrook. That's why I'm here. It's my mother's idea. You can offer me something and I'll offer you something.'

'I don't get your meaning, Edward.'

'I can do your Saturday morning round. I can collect the bets for you. All you have to do is settle them.'

'What. *You*?'

'Do I look like someone who would break the law? Would you say my bearing was suspicious? Anyway, PC Higton would not arrest me.'

'Why not?' Mr Starsbrook's demeanour and manner had noticeably brightened. 'That bugger would sell his own mother to the devil.'

'Three people in our row know something terrible about him. I can't tell you what it is, so don't ask me. I can start next week, if you want me to.'

Waves of joy and relief appeared to sweep over Mr Starsbrook's face. Even the deep frown line between the top of his nose and his eyebrows seemed to become less defined. His face was usually unexpressive on account of his years spent in the company of Bridget Casey but now it spoke. At last, he snapped his fingers as though he were breaking some spell which had held him captive.

'Spot on! It's a spot on idea. Now, about your wages.' Mr Starsbrook wrote out the sum on a scrap of paper and gave it to Edward for approval. It was double what Edward had received from the bread round. 'Or if you like, Eddie, you can take ten per cent of the profits. I should warn you that on some Saturdays I make a loss, and it would mean you got nothing on those days, but bad days like that are few and far between.'

'I'll take the ten per cent, please.'

'Clever choice, lad. You'll be better off with it than the other. But it wasn't for me to make the decision for you.'

'There's just one more thing to remember. My parents don't know anything about this, officially. So better not mention it to them, okay?'

'Understood, Eddie. Quite understood, lad.'

Edward stood and extended his hand towards Mr Starsbrook for a handshake that was tantamount to a contract. He agreed to call round the following Saturday morning at eight-thirty. Mr Starsbrook accompanied him part of the way down the garden path before joining Bridget in the cabbage patch. Edward was enthralled with their communication with each other. The hand signing and gesticulation was beautiful to behold. It was a secret language without words. If the opportunity had arisen he would have dropped Latin at school and replaced it with deaf and dumb signing.

As Edward walked home he checked to see if there was anyone about. Then he lifted one arm, then another and sniffed under each of his armpits. There and then he decided that when he knew Mr Starsbrook better he might suggest to him how refreshing a dab of talcum powder was when applied to certain parts. After he had completed his self-inspection, he hastened his step. Had he left the cap off the tin of his mother's scented apple blossom powder? He'd better find this out before she got back.

After his sandwiches and cake, Edward changed from his clothes into the oldest he could find. When the two of them got home, he would surprise them. He loved to see his father express pleasure and he knew that a little fresh watercress with a little bread and cheese was something his father delighted in. The fishermen he passed along the canal bank nodded a silent greeting to his presence as he walked by. Eventually he came to the fast surging overflow and then followed its course as it cascaded down the canal bank. On reaching the foot of the bank the water had formed a small pool. The main outlet fed a swollen stream which made its way back along the bottom of the canal bank. A small tributary led around a copse of hazel and elder trees. These were now carpeted with bluebells and once Edward had paddled across the stream and stepped on to the wooded side of the bank, the scent of the flowers was about him. They were mentioned in his poem and, for some odd reason, he tried to avoid stepping on a single plant, almost as though he was seeking to avoid murdering someone.

The stream seemed little more than a trickle now, but

Edward was certain of his way. He had been here with Lawrence. Like the owl's nesting site, this was one of Lawrence's rural secrets. At the further end of the wood, two other streams joined the one he had followed and the flow ballooned into a sizeable elbow shape before becoming one body of water on the other side. There were footprints in the mud and there were still clumps of the year's first watercress, dark green and shining, waiting to be picked.

'Don't pull at the plant, Eddie. Break it off at the stalks. If you pull the plants by the roots you'll destroy the whole bed,' Lawrence had said.

Edward recalled these words as he plunged his hands into the cold water again and again until he could barely feel his fingertips. He managed to glean a good bunch without harming the bed and felt content and satisfied as he held the food in both of his hands. He lingered about the spot for some time after his task was complete and sat on a piece of rotting log, listening to the water and the sounds of the wood, and then realised that he was quietly waiting for another arrival.

'Do the footprints in the mud belong to Lawrence? I wish he'd come now. At this moment. I don't know why . . .'

And yet Edward knew that Lawrence would not come. Somehow he celebrated the yearning in the same way that sometimes he longed for things to be different from what they were. In his imaginings, the foliage of hazel leaves nearby would part and Lawrence would emerge.

'I knew I'd find you here, Eddie. I've been thinking about you all day.'

He stood at Edward's side and placed his arm about his shoulders then sat down on the log beside him and . . . Edward's answering gaze, blinded by fantasy, now

84

saw the fat, grey-blue woodlice scuffle haphazardly about the rotten, flaking wood. No. It would never be like that with Lawrence. Would it ever be like that with anyone? He glanced once more at the two sets of footprints, his own and someone else's, then left the spot with the same degree of reverence that believers showed when they departed from a church.

The cups and saucers were ready, the teapot stood beside the kettle, the caddy, sugar bowl and milk were all close to hand. Edward noted the time and knew his parents would arrive at the back gate within five or ten minutes unless a bus had broken down. His father's punctuality could never be questioned. In fact, it could be boring at times. His reliability was such that it never allowed for any element of surprise. He saw him now, opening the gate for his mother, ushering her forward in front of him. Edward clicked the switch down on the electric kettle as they entered the house.

She always looked more tired than usual on these Sundays, and always gave out an air of being pre-occupied, paying less attention to domestic detail and a curious unconcern with what was going on in the room she sat in. Edward didn't mind this, as her critical observations with regard to him were lost in other thoughts. His father would minister to her as though she had returned from some long journey or some extended absence or even as if she had just come home from hospital.

'Now sit yourself down, Esther.' He would pull the chair out for her. 'Let me take your coat. I know where to hang it. You just sit yourself down.'

Edward bided his time, hovered quietly near the sideboard, poured out their tea. His father announced that he would have a little bread and cheese, his mother suggested that he might like a pickled onion or two with

85

it. At this point Edward chose to intervene.

'You can have some watercress if you like, Dad.'

'We haven't got any, and you know it, Edward. What have you been up to?' His mother's question was wide-ranging but suspicious. Now she gave him her full attention as though she were a police constable questioning a suspected delinquent. She tilted her head to one side. 'Wouldn't we all like a bit of watercress? Perhaps if I was Houdini or Jesus Christ I could produce some from thin air.'

'Close your eyes,' Edward commanded and he bent and opened the sideboard cupboard door.

'Keep out of there. How many times have I told you . . .'

'Close your eyes,' Edward shouted and, in one swift movement, he transferred the plate of watercress from its place of hiding on to the table. 'There.'

'What a feast, our Edward. Where did you find this?' His father rubbed his hands with pleasure. When he was pleased, he showed it with the openness of a small child.

'I can't tell you, Dad. It's a secret place. I'm sworn not to tell of it.'

'Fair enough. If there's more than one or two that knows about a watercress bed, it won't last for very long. Soon we'll have none at all.' He took a spring from the plate and munched it. 'Very good. *Very* good.'

His mother helped herself, first shaking a little salt over the leaves.

'I like it as it is, without bread. You can taste the iron in the leaves.' She nodded as she chewed and savoured the stuff. 'This isn't going to make any difference, you know. I've spoken to your father about it. No Saturday job, no school. It's as simple as that.' She took another sprig of cress from the plate.

'I've got another job. It pays better.'

Edward's quick, unconcerned response caused her to pause with the watercress held between her fingers an inch or so from her mouth.

'What? What did you say?'

'You never gave me time to explain myself before. You just flew off the handle before I could tell you about it. You didn't think I would pack in one job without having got another one? Surely not?'

'Now don't play that wide-eyed, innocent, goody two-shoes with me, Edward. I've seen that butter-wouldn't-melt-in-your-mouth look before.' At last she bit off a little of the cress then added. 'What job? What work are you about to start next Saturday morning?'

His father remained an interested but silent observer. He had witnessed these contests between his wife and son on so many occasions. If possible, he sought not to intervene. If he did, he managed to upset one or the other of them. This conflict of two powerful personalities both fascinated and saddened him. Both contestants could be unkind to one another and it was only when he thought that one was being grossly unfair that he assumed the role of referee. If possible, he chose to be a loving spectator.

Edward sighed very audibly with the same kind of gentle exasperation that young mothers offered irrational offspring.

'I'm working with Mr Starsbrook. Giving him clerical assistance.'

'Do I hear right? Are you telling us that as from next Saturday you are going to be a bookie's runner?' His mother's harsh questioning tone had softened and now there was even a trace of admiration in her voice.

'I said I was assisting Mr Starsbrook. I never said

precisely what I was going to do. Officially, neither of you knows.'

'But we do know, our Edward. You're going to collect bets. Starsbrook can add up and settle a wager quicker than anyone in this village. He doesn't need your help to do that.' His father shook his head. 'You could end up at the magistrate's court and then you'd have to leave your present school. They'd have no truck with you if you landed up in that kind of trouble. You'd be breaking the law.'

'If I don't take the job, I'll have to leave school anyway.' Edward nodded to his mother in mock supplication. 'If I do take it, I can stay on. I won't get summonsed anyway. You know that, don't you, Mam?'

'Let him do it. PC Higton won't arrest him, even if he knows he's doing it. He's got more than two blind eyes when it suits him. Suppose there's at least two women in this row of houses who would silence him if needs be.'

'It's a daft law anyway,' his father murmured. He was relieved that this potentially explosive situation had been resolved. Sometimes it felt as though the two of them were talking time-bombs.

Edward suggested to his father that he might like to hear his recitation for the pending poetry competition.

'Oh no, oh no. Not again. He's been driving me bloody mad with his *toll no bell* for this and *toll no bell* for that. He can go upstairs and practise or go outside.'

His mother quickly sabotaged Edward's rehearsal and his father lamely suggested that he wasn't too keen on poems.

'The trouble with you, mother,' Edward spoke as he put on his school blazer and cap. 'The trouble with you is—'

'Now, Edward. I won't have you being sharp-tongued with your mam.'

'No no. Let him have his say. I'd like to know what my trouble is, I really would.'

'You are fixed.' Edward half turned towards her as he reached the door. Her response surprised him. She spoke resignedly, as though admitting some great crime for the first time.

'Maybe you are right. Mmm. Mmm. You could well be right.'

His father patted the back of her hand as if to offer a condolence that he knew carried no lasting balm.

In the past few months it was not unusual for Edward to take solitary walks. The countryside that was all about him offered him a privacy he could not attain elsewhere. His father's general enthusiasm for the landscape and Lawrence's more detailed scrutiny of what grew and lived in it (newts' bellies were the same colour as the inside of foxgloves, for instance) had infected Edward's being. His walks were pleasantly melancholic as from an early age he had wanted to leave both his home and his village and his recent wanderings were always tinged with a kind of regret as though his private strolls were all part of some protracted farewell.

During the war years, in his second year at infants' school, he had asked his teacher if she would put his name down on the list of children to be evacuated.

'But Edward, no-one is being evacuated from this region,' his teacher had sought to reassure him.

'Oh, I know. But if they do start sending children away, can I be first on the list?'

Much to Edward's surprise, the teacher had become tearful and kissed him on the forehead and then given him an apple. Eventually she said, 'No-one is going to be sent away, Edward.'

After rounding a bend in the pot-holed lane, Edward followed the line of a dusty, ochre-coloured track which eventually led him into acres and acres of heath land. Here, the outlook was completely foreign in comparison with his earlier watercressing expedition. The air was strongly scented and spiced with the perfume of heather and pine. He breathed in deeply and gazed at the great splodges of pale purple flowers that erupted between bracken and fern. Here and there stunted silver birch trees struggled towards the sky and clumps of yellow broom grew out from sandy, shale-ridden banks with all the audacity of cactus blooms in the middle of the desert. At the end of each distant horizon, pine trees grew.

Edward enjoyed the harshness of the setting. He felt explorative here as there was no indication of human settlement or influence, no-one farming, no-one fishing, no telegraph wires, not even a pit stack in sight. He memorised and rehearsed his poem, speaking out loudly and fearlessly above the buzzing of insects and bees foraging amongst the heather beneath his feet and the odd clacking noise of a pair of loving magpies overhead.

Assured that he was word perfect, he quickened his pace along the sand track. He heard the noise and the voices before he saw the two men. He did not slow his steps but continued in the same pattern until he reached the spot where the height and weight of a silver birch tree had caused it to topple and uproot itself. Its main trunk and foliage were now sprawled across the track. Two young men worked at either end of the fallen tree. At its base, one was busy sawing the roots from the trunk. At the other end, the second one was using a hatchet to chop away the upper branches and excess foliage. They conversed in staccato fashion, not pausing from their labour which they went about with the kind of concentration a surgeon might find useful. They did not acknowledge Edward's presence because they were unaware that he was standing just a few yards from them.

Edward stood as if transfixed. He had never known why older boys emitted wolf whistles and stared at some girls in gawping admiration. At this moment, he felt scarcely able to breathe, let alone whistle, yet he was filled with a tingling sense of . . . was it admiration?

The two men had discarded their jackets and trousers and were working in white vests and football shorts. Almost gradually, like the spread of ink on blotting paper, Edward's gaze was drawn to different aspects of their physicality. The hair that seemed to bubble from their legs, the line of the arm to the shoulder and the dark patches of hair underneath the arm pits, the strong, thick-set necks and the movement and shape of their dicks beneath the thin cotton of their shorts. The muscles on their forearms stood out beneath the flesh and Edward contemplated the strength of these arms and –

'Nice evenin'.' The one with the saw had paused and placed one foot upon the trunk of the tree. 'Nice evenin'.'

'Oh. It is. It is.' Edward's response seemed to come from somewhere in the back of his head.

'We'll get five bob for this lot when we've finished logging it. I reckon it's cheap at half the price considering the amount of work in it. Still. It passes the time.' He winked and smiled to reveal a single gap in teeth which were otherwise perfect. Hitching up his shorts and revealing the line of his prick still more clearly, he then recommenced his work.

Edward wanted to stay longer and just look at them but felt suddenly overwhelmed by the feelings which had assaulted him. He mumbled a 'cheerio' and swiftly backtracked along the path in the same way that he had come. Sister Bessie at the Baptist Chapel had said that young men who lusted after women were on a one-way ticket to Hell.

'Well,' Edward thought. 'If you are bound for Hell for lusting after women, you can hardly expect to go to Heaven for lusting after men.'

And how was it possible to lust after somebody you'd only just seen?

'Why, you don't even know them. And if you knew them and still lusted after them . . . is that being in love? Or is it romance?'

What was more, he had often heard youths going on about girls' tits, girls' legs and even their bums, but he'd never heard of one admiring other men's dicks.

'I'm different. I'm a changeling. Just like in the poem,' he thought.

He felt bewildered. But not ashamed.

CHAPTER EIGHT

From start to finish the assembly could not have taken longer than fifteen minutes, of which time-span routine and ritual accounted for two-thirds. Five hundred or so boys were marshalled into rows in the hall by prefects. The head prefect clapped his hands together three times and then, apart from a little coughing, there was silence. Major Daventry, the headmaster, led his staff down the central aisle of the hall and up on to the stage. As far as Edward knew, there was no prescribed uniform for members of staff, yet there was very little variation in their dress. All the men wore suits or sports jackets and grey flannel trousers, all wore their academic gowns, some of which were tattered with age, and all of them had striped ties as if in defiance of more fashionably decorative neckwear. The one exception was the art teacher, who wore a corduroy jacket and a yellow bow tie. On a more imposing man this might have achieved a blow for non-conformity but this particular teacher looked somewhat bedraggled and vaguely ridiculous.

They sang *Immortal Invisible* accompanied on the piano by Mrs Daventry, the headmaster's wife. This was immediately followed by the Lord's Prayer, chanted at a cracking pace. Even the Amen came after *forever and ever* without so much as a pause. Major Daventry then announced that the recitation competition would be held during the lunch hour. Three finalists were to be shortlisted and each of these would recite their poem for the rest of the school at a special evening assembly at a quarter to four in the afternoon.

The judges were two English masters and the headmaster's wife, who was known to take a keen interest in the arts. The prizewinner was to receive a postal order for ten shillings, the second, seven shillings and sixpence, and the third, five shillings. This announcement had aroused whispers of envious interest from the hall and there were many boys present who wished they had taken the trouble to nominate themselves before the list had been closed. As things stood, there were twelve boys in competition of the three prizes. It was something quite new for artistic endeavour to be rewarded with cash and Edward felt that if he only achieved a third prize, the payment would be a bargain. As far as he was concerned, there was nothing vulgar about competing for money.

'Thank you, Warrington. The three prizewinners will be announced at tonight's assembly.' There was no trace of approval from the senior English teacher, who was known to be more interested in talking about cricket than literature. Edward had never heard him mention a play or a film and the only book which seemed to set him alight was Jerome K. Jerome's *Three Men in a Boat*. He was known to be a bachelor – a middle-aged one at that. He was tall, square-jawed and would have been considered attractive in some quarters, yet his eyes and facial expression lacked any trace of animation. He sometimes laughed at his own jokes. He was known to favour particular boys and would always ask them to read or show them some subtle kind of personal interest. In lesson times, he always ignored Edward and even now, as he addressed him, this teacher had dead eyes.

'Codfish. He's a piece of codfish,' Edward thought.

'You've had your lunch, have you, Warrington?' the younger English teacher enquired.

'No, Sir. The Ws are always at the end of the line. I think I'm the last competitor.'

'Do you want us to reverse alphabetical order?' The teacher, pale-faced and prematurely bald, managed a thin smile. He glanced at his watch. 'Well, you have another fifteen minutes. You should manage it.'

Edward felt as if his feet had taken root. Surely they were going to say something. Say he'd tried hard, or even that the choice of poem wasn't suitable, or something about the metre. Ask him something about the poem's meaning and what he felt about it. For some reason, his attention was drawn to the sleeves and elbows of their sports jackets, which were protected with leather covering. There and then he decided, he knew, he could never respect either of these men ever again.

'I might as well be pissing against the wind for all these two care. They don't want to be here, let alone listening to any poetry.' Edward mulled this over. Should he say thank you and then leave? No. He'd just nod his head. Such discourtesy would be mild compared with the reception they had given him.

It was left to the non-professional member of the panel to offer some observation with regard to Edward's efforts.

'I thought it was a most original choice, Edward and I felt you had a great feeling for it.' The two men gave Mrs Daventry only half their attention as she spoke, as though she were speaking out of turn in some way. She removed her tortoiseshell glasses as if to indicate that she would not be bullied. 'Yes. A most original rendering,' she added.

Edward breathed in deeply, met her unspectacled gaze

and said, 'Thank you, Mrs Daventry. Thank you.' He smiled in her direction without a trace of sycophancy, nodded to the two men and left.

He collected his lunch and sat alone in the dining hall. The cooks had been generous so that his plate was piled high with mashed potatoes and a meat course which contained a high proportion of bones. It may have been lamb or mutton once upon a time, but here at school it was referred to as churchyard stew. He ate at a leisurely pace. He had no intention of bolting his food down. He knew he would be late for the commencement of the afternoon lesson time. He was unconcerned about this as there always seemed to be time to spare during art lessons.

As he sucked the flesh off each and every bone, he imagined how marvellous it would be if Mrs Daventry were his mother. She would play the piano for him, buy him books and greet him with maternal kisses and tenderness when he arrived home. She'd let him have a bath every day and he'd use Palmolive soap, not the red blocks of carbolic.

'Prunes and custard?'

'Is there anything else?' Edward had returned his dinner plates and cutlery. His enquiry carried a polite, hopeful inflection.

'There was some jam tart but it has all gone.' Noting the disappointment on Edward's face, the dinner lady added. 'They're good for you. Prunes keep you regular.'

'I'm allergic to them. The last time I had them they affected me so badly the doctor thought I had dysentery. I was on the toilet *all night*.' Edward lied unashamedly. He had found that when someone said something was *good* for you, it tasted horrible. Anyway, who wanted medicine for afters?

His fantasy illness won him the piece of jam tart that

he knew existed somewhere in the kitchen. He ate it quickly and made his way out. He crossed the playground, ascended the wooden stairs that led up to the art room and arrived at his lesson twenty minutes late.

'I've been taking part in the poetry competition, Sir. Mr Burton, Mr Trafford and Mrs Daventry told me to go for my lunch before coming on here. I was the last entry to be called in. I'm to give you their apologies for my lateness, Sir.' Edward knew there would be no opposition to this formidable staff trio and, like the other boys, he considered the art teacher to be an idle man. His alibi would not be checked.

'You are to design a poster for one of the following events.' With a disinterested gesture, the teacher referred Edward to the large blackboard behind him. 'Remember time, place and lettering are all important. You are to use powder paint and grey sugar paper. Understood?'

'Yes, Sir.' Edward wasted no time taking his place behind an empty easel. His art teacher took no further notice and returned to studying the book in front of him as he was deeply involved in local amateur dramatics and had been widely praised in the local paper for his performances in *Rookery Nook, Murder at the Vicarage*, and *Quiet Wedding*.

A Swimming Gala, A Circus, A Holiday Resort. Two of these subjects held some appeal for Edward but he chose that which had the least for his exercise. He'd once seen a film about a circus. He'd laughed at the clowns, felt terrible when a trapeze artist had come to terrible grief after a fall from a great height, and been thoroughly miserable to see the huge but beautiful elephants walking around on their hind legs. The comedy and tragedy were too close in this form of entertainment and the net result had left Edward feeling disconsolate and unnerved.

'Oughtn't your clown have a little more colour to him? Perhaps a little orange would give the blue some sharper tones.' This was one of the three peremptory trawls the art teacher took in the space of the one and a half hour lesson period. 'Your fellow looks decidedly glum for a clown. Oughtn't he to wear a grin or a smile? He's hardly inviting people to the event, is he?'

'Clowns are often sad-faced, Sir.'

'Surely not.'

'Charlie Chaplin looks sad, Sir and scores of people go to see him. I—'

'Mmm. Mmm. Perhaps. You have the dates, times, place and admission fees. What's missing? You have forgotten a vital piece of information.'

'I don't think I have. I can't see what I have missed out.'

'Does this event have a name?' the teacher questioned in a triumphalist, superior manner. Response of any kind or even no response would be rewarded with belittlement. Edward extended his forefinger and dotted each one of the six circles which formed an arc about the figure.

'Every ball will carry a letter. S-M-A-R-T-S C-I-R-C-U-S.'

'What is he doing with those balls?'

There were sniggers from some of his classmates. Edward was aware of this trap. If he lost his composure and laughed, it would mean a detention.

'He's juggling with them, Sir.'

'What? Six of them?'

'Some jugglers can manage eight balls, Sir.' Edward picked up his paint brush and remained stony-faced. He caught a whiff of stale pipe tobacco as the teacher passed by him to offer untelling criticism to the boy working behind.

Fifteen minutes before the closure of the lesson, the

teacher made his final patrol about the room. Each pictorial effort was granted a grade. Most ranged from C minus to C plus, as the teacher had a strong belief in artistic average. On this particular visit, he managed to bring some individuality into his judgement by asking each boy a personal question which had nothing to do with their efforts in art.

'C. C. No. I'll make it C plus, Evans. There's evidence of care in the lettering. And what does your father do?'

'He's a retail ironmonger, Sir. We have two shops. One here and one in Burton-on-Trent.'

'I'll know where to come, then, if I ever run short of a nail or hammer.'

Edward could smell the man but did not turn to give him an expectant look as if he were some respectful serf in the presence of royalty.

'I see you granted your clown a smile after all, Warrington. Yet he still looks a trifle baleful. The lettering is a little shaky but the poster has originality. Yes. A B minus for that.' He spoke regretfully, as thought he were saddened by offering a grade slightly beyond a C. 'And what does your father do?'

'He's a coal-miner, Sir.'

'Oh really?' the teacher exclaimed. 'Is he involved in colliery management?'

'No, Sir. He works on the coal-face. He is a coal-cutter.'

'Good Lord, and is he pleased that you are here with us? You're not local, are you?'

Edward ignored the first question.

'I'm from Ardmoor, Sir, near Batsford. Most men are coal-miners in our village.'

'If he says he'll come to my home for a bucket of coal, I'll tell him I'll bounce a lump off the top of his head if he does,' thought Edward. He had found that, like his father, he could be very defensive about his village or coal-miners if people from the outside made observations about the insularity of such communities. The way this man talked, you would think he might need a passport to visit Ardmoor or that Edward was an Aborigine or something like that.

The evening assembly was a rarity. Usually these only took place at the end of term, when Major Daventry always wished the boys a good and trouble-free holiday and then stated that he'd expect them back at school like *giants refreshed*. Then they sang *Lord Dismiss Us* and all the school got away pretty quickly after that, the Lord's will, for once in a while, being strictly adhered to.

There was a *frisson* of excitement due to a mixture of this novel gathering in the middle of the term and the sensational innovation of a boy being honoured for saying a poem. Boys had mounted the rostrum for excellence at cricket, athletics, even a university placement, but for a recitation? Everyone felt that Mrs Daventry was the inspiration behind this venture but no-one had any real proof that this was so. She sat there, smiling in a floral print dress. On either side of her sat the two English masters who looked as though they were waiting for a dental appointment. Major Daventry took the centre of the stage and raised his hand and at this signal all whispering within the hall ceased.

'The judges have reached their conclusions with regard to the verse-speaking competition. I shall read out the names of the prizewinners beginning with the third prize and so on. Each prizewinner will speak his verse to the school when he has ascended the platform.'

More whispers and chatter followed this announcement. This bit of the proceedings hadn't been written into the original terms of the competition and few of the twelve boys who had entered now wished to hear their names reverberate around the hall. Major Daventry lifted his hand and the chatter ceased once more.

'The third prizewinner is . . .' He paused, caught up in his own schoolmasterly histrionics. 'The third prizewinner is Roland Costello of Form IIIB.'

This announcement was greeted by gasps from the hall. A boy from a B class was hardly ever mentioned in terms of accolade and Roland was hardly considered to be an integral part of the school. What was more, he didn't seem to mind not being part of it. Nothing that went on here ever seemed to be his central interest. He had a reputation for being lax about doing his homework and no interest whatsoever in sport. His record of occasional days' absences was the worst in the school and he never seemed to be concerned about this either. Detentions had proved useless when doled out for him not suffering a short back and sides haircut. He wore his hair longer than anyone and had cultivated a DA that any of the town's Teddy boys would have envied.

'Make your way forward, Costello.' Major Daventry peered over his half-moon glasses. Roland Costello made his way up to the platform as though he had been doing it every day of the week instead of this being the first time. When he received his postal order, he raised it above his head and managed to milk a little more applause. Anyone would think he was winning an Academy Award rather than the third prize. Yet still, Edward admired him now as he calmly brushed both sides of his hair into place with his hands and took centre-stage.

'A sonnet by William Shakespeare.'

Edward's attention was now fully focused on Roland. Feet slightly apart, hands clutching his thighs, chin uplifted, Roland's eyes looked out somewhere beyond the three, high-arched windows which took up most of the back part of the hall. His stance and posture seemed to indicate that he was unaware of an audience.

'To His Love.'

The title, so boldly declared, caused Edward to catch his breath in anticipation of what was to follow. The two English teachers sitting behind Roland seemed to be examining their ties. Surely they couldn't disapprove of Shakespeare? It would be heresy. But Edward noted that they looked far from appreciative.

> *'Sometime too hot the eye of Heaven shines,*
> *And often is his gold complexion dimm'd:*
> *And every fair from fair sometime declines*
> *By chance, or nature's changing course, untrimm'd'*

'I'm listening to a *love* poem about a man for another man. At least that's how Roland is interpreting it. Or is it just me?' thought Edward, who had felt the blood rush into his neck and face as the full import of the poem and its brave delivery seemed to enter his very being. He felt both relief and elation. 'I'm *not* the only person in the world who has felt these things. I don't have to live alone when I'm older . . . And if . . .'

> *'So long as men can breathe, or eyes can see,*
> *So long lives this, and this gives life to thee.'*

Applause came generously after the final lines. Edward had never clapped anything so vigorously in all his life. In fact, he was bursting to lead some cheers. The English teachers on the platform had barely brought their hands together more than two or three times. All the boys in the B stream supported Roland by prolonging the applause and Roland looked towards

his own class for the first time and smiled in an arrogant
kind of way as if he knew something which they didn't,
almost as if he felt sorry for them in some way. With a
slight wave of the hand, Major Daventry ushered him
to the side of the platform and Mrs Daventry spoke a
few personal words to him and smiled.

Edward's thoughts were entirely centred on what had
gone before. Major Daventry was speaking but Edward
gave little heed to what was being said. All ideas that
there was more to follow seemed to have been marooned
in another part of his brain. He was aware of the wave
of applause, but had missed the announcement.

'It's you.' Edward was brought back to his present
reality by a sharp dig in the ribs. 'Go on, Edward. It's
you!' the boy sitting next to him said and then whispered
loudly. 'You're second.'

The walk from his place in the hall down the central
aisle seemed endless. Edward kept his eyes fixed forward
and centred his gaze on Mrs Daventry's floral print
dress. He was surprised to find that no traces of
apprehension or nervousness assailed him. If anything,
he felt justified and calm and oddly cut off from this
centre-stage experience. It was more like having a part
in a film than something that was really happening.

He received his postal order from Major Daventry,
who smiled welcomingly and seemed genuinely pleased
that Edward had won it. Edward made no gesture of
triumph to his fellow pupils as Roland had done, but
before he began his recitation, he extended his right hand
to Mrs Daventry who clasped it in both her hands,
squeezed it and muttered, 'I'm so glad for you, Edward.'

He looked at his audience before he began and then,
after announcing the title, forgot they were there. The
poet's words became his words and there were no
problems for him in recalling or delivering them. After

the applause had faded, he stood next to Roland on the platform.

The thoughts of both boys were in tandem. If they were the runners-up in this competition, then the winner was bound to offer something electrifying in content. By the usual standards, surprise had never been the order of the day in school assemblies and here, today, one shock result had been followed by another, and there was still one more to come. Who would win? What was the poem going to be about?

'The first prize goes to A. V. Fosberry of the Upper Sixth.'

Major Daventry's announcement was met with tepid, polite applause, which suggested a degree of disappointment rather than spontaneous good will. Edward patted his hands together in a lame fashion but Roland's remained glued to his sides. Andrew Fosberry was the oldest boy in the school. He was completing an extra year after his eighteenth birthday in order to resit one of the papers in his advanced certificate. It was well known that he intended a career for himself in the army. Not as a soldier, but as an officer. He had adopted a military bearing from his early teens and in his communication with other boys, his posture always seemed somewhat stiff and his conversation monosyllabic. For the past two years, he had been successful in initiating a cadet corps within the school which was attended by ten to fourteen boys who dressed up for the occasion in adolescent battledress. They met on Thursday evenings, marched around the playground, blew on a trumpet and saluted the Union Jack which fluttered from the old Church Tower. No-one ever used A.V. Fosberry's Christian name. If they had, he would have accused them of being a cissy. He had become an adult without ever having seemed to have experienced childhood. By the time he was twenty-one, he would look and behave as if he were closer to forty.

Edward watched the tall, thin, sharp-featured young man stand to attention on the front of the stage as if he were on a parade ground. Feet the regulation distance apart, arms and hands to the side. Both sides of the mouth were decorated with acne. The thin, inexpressive lips moved to make an announcement whose words were delivered in a monotone.

'The following is an extract from *The Times* and the incident it describes is the subject matter for this poem. *Some Sikhs and a private of the Buffs having remained behind with grog carts, fell into the hands of the Chinese. On the next morning they were brought before the authorities and commanded to perform the "Kowtow". The Sikhs obeyed; but Moyse, the English soldier, declaring that he would not prostrate himself before any Chinaman alive, was immediately knocked upon the head, and his body thrown on a dung hill.*'

Edward wasn't sure if they were all supposed to feel sorry for this poor soldier, who surely must have been drunk, or to despise his arrogance or stupidity. He blinked as A.V. Fosberry brought his heels together with a click and raised his right hand to his brow in salute.

'*The Private of the Buffs.*'

Five verses followed, swiftly delivered in a voice void of modulation or inflection. Not until the last line was delivered did the militaristic stance relax. Through the polite applause, Roland Costello muttered through clenched teeth, 'Who the hell does he think he is? General Custer?'

'Silly bugger,' Edward replied and clapped simultaneously, as he spoke only for Roland's ears.

'Even if we run all the way, we won't catch the first

train.' Roland had stopped hurrying and paused in front of a shop window which displayed bridal gowns. 'My mother says most of the girls who marry in Batsford aren't entitled to wear white.'

'Why not?' Edward asked.

'She says they've had sexual intercourse with the men before they have the wedding rings on their fingers. I can't blame them though. How could you marry someone without knowing what they are like? I mean, they might smell between the legs or snore. Did your mother marry in white?'

'I don't know,' Edward replied truthfully. 'What about yours?'

'Oh no. She was a farmer's daughter. She was carrying my older brother around at the time.'

'What? In her arms?'

'No, stupid. In her belly. She was seven months gone. She had to get married.'

'Who told you this, Roland? It might not be true.' Edward attempted to offer some comfort but it was wasted.

'She did. We talk about everything.' Roland spoke in a wearied, adult manner and Edward felt a little squashed in the presence of such maturity.

The two of them had been the last to leave the hall after ten minutes of courteous chat with Mrs Daventry. They both knew the cost of politeness was to arrive home some time just before seven pm. They had known each other for barely twenty minutes when Edward began to feel something close to a miracle had occurred as it seemed as though they had known each other all their lives. They talked and talked as though language and communication skills had only just been conferred on them; each felt as though the other was related to him in some way.

'I never expected to be second after I heard you,' Edward opined generously. 'It's good the third year took both place prizes.'

'You should have won. Or I should. The most fair result would have been for us to share the first prize. Me for presentation and style and you for charm and originality. How they could pick A.V. Fosberry as the winner I don't know. Well. I do know why that streak of piss won and it's got nothing to do with poetry. His father is a freemason and so is that boring fart of an English teacher. I'm having the day off tomorrow.'

'Are you going to a funeral?' Edward ventured carefully.

'Funeral? Are you mad? Of course not. I'm spending the day with my mother.'

'Oh. I suppose you're going to help out on the farm. It must be great having so much space and animals and things.'

'I wouldn't know. We keep a public house. The Dog and Cat. It's in Great Myrton.'

'You live even further away than me then. I'm in Ardmoor. Is your mother sick?'

'No. I am. Sick to the back teeth of that hick joint we call school.'

'You sound like Barbara Stanwyck. She talks like that.'

'Isn't she marvellous?' Roland responded quickly and Edward nodded enthusiastically.

They had to stop walking every four or five minutes as the beginnings of an evening breeze began to dislodge Roland's cap which was perched, rather than worn, on the back of his head. The front of his hair fell in a Tony Curtis quiff on to his brow and, what with side waves and a splendid DA, there was little room for head gear.

Edward was a little taken aback as Roland carried a

case. No-one else in the third year demonstrated such audacity. A satchel had to be borne on your shoulder until you were in the Upper Fifth. After that a case would be deemed in order. It seemed to be a demarcation point from being a schoolboy to becoming a student, an accessory that only the more mature could carry. It was an unwritten rule, but everyone seemed to obey it, except Roland. And surely the stories and rumours about his neglectful attitude towards homework couldn't possibly be true? Roland's case looked larger than any other Edward had seen. There would be no point in carrying a case that size to and fro to school every day unless there were plenty of books in it.

There was still a wait of twenty-five minutes before the second train was due to leave Trentvale for Batsford. Roland walked past a group of four or five boys who had suffered the ignominy of a detention and motioned Edward to follow him to the other end of the platform.

'We don't want to stand with that lot. They're all in my class and they'll talk about football and want us to play whist with them. They're common. Dead common.'

Edward soon realised that no sporting activity of any kind should be mentioned to Roland.

'Surely you like swimming,' he had bravely asserted after Roland had listed all the despicable effects of football, hockey and cricket on someone like himself.

'I like floating in the bath at home. If you swim in the Trent you'll get mastoids in your ears as well as risking a fever if you dive under water. Do you swim? Who taught you?'

'I just learned with the other boys in my village. In the canal. I think I could swim when I was seven.'

'The canal. God, you're lucky to be still alive! If you'd been born in Africa, you would most likely have gone blind.'

There was even less success for Edward when he had tried to point out some of the good things about their school. There was no bullying, no corporal punishment. He listed at least four teachers who were extremely kind. In some areas, like history and geography, the teachers were brilliant and –. Roland had dismissed Edward's counsel for the defence with a wave of the hand.

'I don't believe in schools. Not of any kind.'

'But how would you ever learn anything?' Edward had become a little exasperated as even at this relatively early age, he had a genuine love of learning and discovery.

'You could find it all out from books. Or tutors could visit you at home.'

'Not my home, they couldn't,' Edward had glumly asserted.

'Well, you could visit them. It would be your choice. You wouldn't have to be taught English Literature by two dried prunes who would give first prize to A. V. Fosberry honking out *The Private of the Buffs*.'

Edward soon realised that Roland was not averse to doing a little tutoring himself. He delivered isolated chunks of information as though none of it could be questioned. And if you did question anything, he'd get ratty. Jesus's father wasn't a carpenter but a farmer. Susan Hayward had a false leg. Mrs Daventry could have been a famous opera singer if she hadn't chosen to give her body to Major Daventry. And your balls would drop off by the time you were thirty if you didn't have fresh underpants on every day.'

'What if you never wore underpants at all?'

'Don't be ridiculous,' was the retort.

The steam rising in small, white clouds from behind a distant copse heralded the oncoming train. Edward always enjoyed watching the engine come into view and had developed a love of trains. Roland talked on, unaware of its existence.

'I'm sure you won't mind me mentioning it, but you seem not to know when to use the long A.'

'What's *that*?' Edward was confounded.

'Haven't you ever listened to the wireless? I mean the announcers of programmes and people giving out the news. They use the long A and the short A. All your As are short. Most people around here only know of the short A. You'll never get on anywhere else if you don't use the long A.'

Now Edward felt he had to give Roland his full attention. His future career was hazy and vague to him, but he was quite certain he wouldn't stay in Batsford. He couldn't stay. He didn't want to arrive anywhere else handicapped in any way. Roland wasted no time in putting him out of his misery.

'At laaast I'm here on the graaas with you. Bang Crash goes my heart.' He slicked a lock of hair away from his forehead. 'You wouldn't say baaang craaash went my heart, would you?'

'No. You wouldn't,' Edward murmured. If hearts banged and crashed, he thought, you'd be dead, not lying on the grass with a lover. The niceties of standard spoken English still left him somewhat puzzled. He was spared further instruction by the railway engine, which snorted past them before grinding to a halt. Both boys were pleased to find they had a railway compartment to themselves.

As soon as the carriage door was shut, Edward was surprised to see Roland unlacing his shoes and removing them from his feet. As the engine rolled slowly forward, he unknotted his tie and flung it on the seat opposite. His cap he snatched off his head and hurled, discus-fashion, in the same direction. When he began to unbutton his blazer, Edward felt a tremor of concern. Was Roland going to strip naked here in the compartment? Shouldn't they draw the blinds down on the windows? And if they did draw the blinds down, what then?

He found Roland enchanting but not exciting, not sexy in anyway. Yet he was very good-looking. Perhaps too good-looking. Perhaps too aware of his own beauty for him to seem real. Edward looked out of the window in the same way he did when his father was in the tin bath on the hearth.

'Would you like a cigarette?'

'No thanks,' Edward shouted from the half-open carriage window. 'If he's naked when I turn around,' he thought, 'I'll say I've got some grit in my eye. Say I'm in agony.' Desperate situations needed desperate remedies. The approaching entrance of the tunnel hardened Edward's resolve.

The undressing had continued at a steady but not yet alarming pace. Roland was now barefooted. His discarded grey stockings lay close to his tie and cap on the seat opposite. At the point where Edward was going to claim his eye injury, Roland stretched up and heaved his case off the luggage rack. He clicked the catches open and said, 'At last, I can be myself.'

Edward watched as Roland emptied the case. There was not a textbook or an exercise book in sight, not even a ruler or a pencil. The case seemed to be full of clothes. Roland took out a pair of brightly coloured turquoise socks and wrongly described them as being duck-egg blue.

'My mother says the colour matches my eyes.' Roland slipped the second sock over his left foot. 'What do you think?'

'I think those socks are closer to the colour of thrushes' eggs.' He noted the beginnings of a frown on

Roland's brow and quickly added. 'But the colour is very complimentary.'

Next he encased his feet in a pair of dark green suede shoes with thick soles on the bottom which seemed to increase his height by two inches or so. He adorned his throat with a green and white scarf, paying a great deal of attention to the size of the loose fitting knot and the position of his shirt collar.

'I like your scarf.'

'It's a *cravat*. A well-tied cravat is the first serious step in life. That's a line from a play, you know. I'm going on the stage when I'm older.' Roland looked at his face full-on and in profile as he spoke then bent and took out a yellow woollen zipper jacket with a turtle collar to complete his new wardrobe.

Edward felt as though he had witnessed the pupation of some huge butterfly. He watched the creature now as it neatly packed its discarded coverings into its case and snapped the lid shut.

'There. I wouldn't be seen dead walking around Batsford in that lot.' He seated himself in the opposite corner of the carriage from Edward, took out a cigarette from a packet of ten in his shirt pocket and lit it. After two short puffs, he blew a smoke ring up in the air and followed its ascent with his eyes. 'Do you like Crawford?'

'Who?' Edward felt he might be referring to some boy at school.

'Joan Crawford.'

'Oh yes. Yes I do.' Edward was genuinely enthusiastic.

'I'm going to see her tomorrow afternoon. My mother can only go to matinées. She's got the pub to manage in the evenings.'

'Doesn't she mind you missing school?' Edward found all of this difficult to believe.

'Course not. Why should she? She knows I'm going

on the stage. She'll give me a note. It was tonsillitis and a temperature last week so it will be diarrhoea tomorrow. I've never been sick in my life, you know. Nor have I ever had a mattered pimple or a blackhead. By the way. Away from school, if we meet, don't use the name Roland. Just call me Costello. When I'm on the stage or in films, I'll just have the one name.'

'Costello,' Edward said the name aloud and saw it in neon lights. 'But isn't it the name of a comedian?'

'He'll be dead by the time I'm on the screen,' Costello observed with some irritation.

The train's pace slowed and Costello took this as a signal to check his appearance in the compartment mirror yet again.

'If anyone gets in here at Pine Halt and I start talking to them, remember you are my younger cousin and my name is Andrew and I'm working as a trainee cinema manager in Burton-on-Trent.'

Edward nodded. There was no time to go into the reasons for this subterfuge. It was like being in a spy film, being with Costello. It was very hard knowing what was going to happen next. Who could Costello know from Pine Halt? The only people that ever got on the train there were RAF men from the camp nearby. Costello wouldn't know anyone from there. Or would he? The train halted and Edward felt as if he would burst from tension. Costello blew smoke rings and looked bored. He was a fine actor.

'I think the platform was deserted. No-one got off here either.' Edward glanced out of the window as he spoke. 'Who were you expecting?'

'Oh, nobody in particular. But it's as well to be prepared.' Costello seemed unconcerned.

Edward wondered why Costello couldn't just be himself. But maybe, as he was going to be an actor, he

needed to play many parts. As of now he had somehow
managed to look about sixteen when he was nearer
thirteen. When you were young, you sometimes tried to
look older and when you were older you often tried to
look younger.

'I don't want to be older than nineteen.' It was as if
Costello had read Edward's thoughts. 'I shall give up
birthdays for five years when I'm nineteen.' Edward was
furiously trying to reckon what Costello's true age
would be when he recorded twenty-one but was drawn
from this fascinating exercise in mental arithmetic by
Costello again. 'Why don't you come to the elocution
and drama classes at the Mining College in Batsford?
Every Saturday at the Mining College in Batsford. Half-
past four until half-past six.'

'How much is it?'

'It's free. The teacher is marvellous. Her name's
Belinda Spight. And she trained at the Central School of
Speech and Drama in London. She is casting for parts
in the pageant. Celebrations to be held on Batsford
Heath in the open air. Don't you want to be part of the
Festival of Britain?'

'I'll see you there, then,' said Edward, who didn't
have to think long about such an enticing invitation.

'You can wear what you like,' Costello looked
disdainfully at Edward's school blazer. 'A polo-necked
jumper would suit you. I might not come into school
much this week at all. My telephone number is Batsford
3295. Can you remember it?' Edward nodded.

'Do you think it's a good idea to have so much time
off school, Costello? They might kick you out if they
knew. Expel you.'

'I don't care if they do.' Costello shrugged his
shoulders in an exaggerated fashion. 'They won't
anyway. I'm FP.'

'FP?'

'Fee paying. If I have days off, why should they worry? They're still being paid. Can you remember the telephone number?'

'Batsford 3295,' Edward spoke it. He had remembered it without any cogitation. It was indelibly imprinted on his mind. He could not admit to Costello that this was the first telephone number he had ever been given. Nor could he state that he had never held the apparatus for communication in his hand. With success in the poetry competition, meeting Costello, future classes in elocution and drama, this had been a wonderful day, full of new and exciting landscapes, and now he was going to speak to someone on the telephone. There seemed to be no end to it all. His home and his mother didn't seem to fit into the present or future scheme of things. Already, he felt that a great part of him had begun to leave the house where he was born.

CHAPTER NINE

'Well, I hope the weather is fine for you, our Edward.' His father surveyed the sky from the back kitchen window. 'It looks clear enough. I'll bet it will be better than anything on down in London. Mr Atlee ought to come up here to see all of you. I never heard tell of a play being done, though, apart from *Punch and Judy* on the sands at Blackpool.'

'It's not *Punch and Judy*, Dad. We are doing *Androcles and the Lion*. There's a cast of a hundred and eighty or more.'

'Good God. It's just as well for the audience you aren't inside a theatre. There'd be no room for them.'

'It's a dress rehearsal today. Our play is only part of the pageant. There are choirs, and Mrs Phelps opens it all riding on a horse.'

'What? Elsie Phelps, our councillor?'

'Yes. She's playing Queen Elizabeth I. She only says a few words.'

'It's just as well, our Edward. I shouldn't think she'll be able to keep her arse in the saddle for more than five minutes. I hope the weather holds for you. It should do. June is supposed to be flaming. Bring in our tea cups. While I'm here, I may as well do them too. The water's still hot enough.'

Mr Warrington passed the last of the breakfast plates to Edward for wiping. It was Saturday. Edward's mother had left early for the market. Unlike many fathers in the village, he did his share of the domestic chores. He would sometimes cook, often wash up the dishes and on Saturdays, during his wife's absence, he would black-lead the grate until it sparkled.

'I'll see you tomorrow, then, Dad.'

Edward heard his father calling, 'Just you be careful, then,' as he closed the back kitchen door behind him.

It was now ten minutes to nine, time for him to collect his bets from his customers. Mr Starsbrook called them *punters* but Edward disliked this word. It didn't seem to fit any of the people he visited. He enjoyed his morning job and because of it he had become popular throughout his village. He entered an adult world which intrigued and beguiled him. In turn, Edward's favourite customers granted him the courtesy due to a young man rather than a teenager.

By special arrangement, his first call was always made on Mrs Settle. Viola Settle was an enormous woman approaching fifty years of age. She lived in a house which was one of four at the bottom of the street in which Edward lived. Her front door was always un-locked, even though she used her front room as a bedroom. She had not moved from this room and her back living room for over three years. She was a sweet-natured, kind woman who knew how to put kindness and sweetness to good use. Since Edward's first call, she had remained a fervent regular.

'I bless the day I set eyes on that boy. He's a treasure. No other word for it. I wait for him like a blackbird hoping for springtime.'

From his first visit, Edward was forever ensnared by her good nature. He had followed Mr Starsbrook's instructions and knocked on the front door.

'Come in. Come in, dear,' a high piping voice had

welcomed him to enter. Mr Starsbrook had urged him
not to hang about but such was Mrs Settle's command-
ing presence, he felt drawn to sit down opposite her.
She sat wedged inside a large chair which had once been
part of a three-piece suite. He had never seen a woman
quite so large in all his life.

She always wore a black dress with buttons straight
down the centre, which stopped at her hemline, below
her calves. Her thick black hair was held in place by a
hairnet which looked as though someone had sprinkled
confetti or cake decorations over it. Her eyes were dark
brown, her complexion sallow and a uniform olive-grey.

There were no distinguishing features to her face as,
like the rest of her, it contained acres of loose flesh. She
had three chins when she held her head erect, but if she
bent forward, they increased to four. At one time
Edward had thought that her dark apparel had been
worn continuously to honour her late husband who had
been dead for over ten years. He had found the idea of
this massive woman wearing funeral clothes for a long
deceased husband mordantly romantic.

'Oh, I tell you, Eddie, I wouldn't want to wish the life
I've had on anybody. Just four days – four days, mark
you – after the war was over, my husband died on me. I
tell you, it's no joy spending half the night in bed with
a dead man, even if he is your husband.'

'You must miss him a lot, Mrs Settle,' he had observed
quietly.

'Oh, no, dear. I can't say that I *miss* him at all. It's
almost as though he was never there, even though I have
three lovely daughters to thank him for, although the
making of them was nothing to write home about, I can
tell you. You see I got all this black material from the
Co-op Hall. It was surplus when the war was over. Black
curtains don't give out much cheer, do they? Ivy, she's

my eldest daughter, is good with the needle. Made me six dresses out of it. I let her have my clothing coupons.' She touched the top of her head. 'All my colour is in my hairnet.'

At first, Edward had been sympathetic in doing what he could to alleviate the terrible anxieties that Mrs Settle suffered from. When one irrational fear disappeared, it was swiftly replaced by another one.

'My nerves are so bad, I'm frightened to close my eyes at night in case I don't wake up in the morning. The doctor says I need a change – suggested I go to holiday camp with my youngest daughter and her husband. The journey would kill me and I could never sleep in a shed. They call them chalets but a shed is a shed no matter how painted up it is.'

Her present fear gave Edward real cause for alarm as he felt there could be some measure of truth in her own dire prognosis of what was going to happen to her.

'I'm sure one day I'll explode. Go off bang. Just like that. It's as though my whole body were a time-bomb. I get such a lot of wind.'

He had suggested it might help if she cut down on food in between her main meals.

'Can't. I can't, duck. Nibbling on something calms my nerves. Have a biscuit, if you want one. Can you cut me a slice of angel cake in the kitchen and bring the chocolate marshmallows in with you. We can have a couple each before you leave.'

Edward always ate what Mrs Settle offered. He felt he was at least reducing her intake a little. Nevertheless, her jaws moved in a slow, steady rhythm for most of the time he was there. In the midst of her generosity, demands were made.

'Could you fill the coal bucket for me, love? I wonder if you'd just give this front window a wipe over. It's my view of the world. I don't ask for much. Rinse those milk bottles and place them outside for me, there's a love . . .'

The first of Mrs Settle's daughters usually arrived before Edward had finished one task or another. All three daughters provided a shuttle service of care and attention. When one left, one arrived, so that she was rarely alone and although she often claimed that she was not long for this world, Edward felt she would probably last longer than her exhausted-looking, dutiful daughters.

For the past three weeks, Edward had managed to improve his own situation as well as cutting down on Mrs Settle's food intake.

'I could lose this leg,' Mrs Settle had patted her left thigh and then pointed towards the heavily bandaged calf with her other hand. 'Ulcers. I've got two beauties. They need dressing three times a day and my youngest daughter can't face it. She's not up to it. Good as gold but not up to it. I hope she won't feel bad if it's amputated.'

Edward had been slightly ashamed at his own thoughts on the matter: 'Well, if she loses one leg, it's not going to make much difference as she never uses either of them.'

He had offered to bandage the leg almost as a penance for his grim conjecture. He had found the task less unpleasant than he imagined. If he took his time over it, Viola was unable to eat and could hardly expect him to do anything else. She had been surprised that he had not been repulsed by the two red, inflamed sores. Indeed, Edward studied them before he applied the dressing and bandages. For him, they were volcanic craters which needed calming and he was qualmless in his treatment of them. When his father had been afflicted with a huge carbuncle on his left buttock, it had been Edward who had applied the kaolin poultice before he had left home for work.

'I'll say this much for you, our Edward. You're not fickle stomached.'

Viola was equally unstinting in her praise.

'I said to my Ivy, *Ivy, that young man does my leg better than Dr Proffit*. I swear to God it's getting better since he's been doing it. That young man's got the touch. He's got the touch.'

Viola's bet rarely varied: one and sixpence each way on the second favourite in the first race, unless there was another horse whose name took her uninformed fancy. Somehow Edward managed to be applying the safety pin to the bandage just as Ivy arrived. He was then able to leave without too much difficulty but not before Viola had delivered a stiflingly loving testimonial.

'Oh, our Ivy, I love that boy so much I could cry! You're a bit late today. It's twenty past the hour. You're usually here at quarter past. Never mind. It's lovely to see you, dear.'

Usually Edward left his longest call until last but he decided to get it over with as the afternoon seemed crowded with events and, if possible, he sought to lop half an hour off his collection time. Dulcie Piper's bungalow had originally been built with the same uniformity as all the council bungalows in her street. Now it stood out from the rest like a cottage belonging to a good fairy or a witch in a Grimm Brothers tale. The front lawn looked like any other lawn except that it was peopled with small statues and figures which Santa Claus or Walt Disney might have considered using but had finally rejected. Gnomes, squirrels, elves, dwarfs, frogs, rabbits, foxes, pixies and one or two coy fairies all fought for space on Dulcie's patch of grass. The serviceable dark green paintwork on the other houses served to emphasise the bright yellow on Dulcie's woodwork. Her front door was of a lilac colour and at its centre was a wrought iron knocker shaped like a cat. Her white netting curtains were tied at the centre with a red bow. As she said herself with some degree of pride, 'If strangers walk down this street, they always pause outside my house.'

A glass lean-to had been attached to the back door. She had asked Edward what he would call this edifice if other people asked about it.

'It's a verandah, Mrs Piper. A verandah. Nobody else in the village has one.' He knew how to please Dulcie.

'No, dear. It's a *conservatory*. If anyone asks, say I've got a conservatory. I can grow grapes, you know. Imagine plucking a bunch of grapes from within your own house.' She would sigh with pleasure after she had made such statements. Domestic improvements always seemed to grant her rapture. There were no framed pictures inside Dulcie's house. Peculiar plaster casts of idyllic cottages bedecked with flowers and women in crinoline dresses dotted the walls and, above the mantelpiece, six multicoloured ducks flew up towards the ceiling.

On his last visit, Dulcie had questioned him almost as soon as he had stepped into the conservatory.

'Did you notice the sign on the gate, Edward?' He shook his head. 'I've named the house. Why should a house like this one have to suffer a number just like everybody else? I'm not number nine anymore, I'm *The Haven*.'

'Do you still keep the number?'

'Why do you think I'd need a number when I have a name? Only people in prison have numbers. Really, Edward, I'd have thought better of you.'

'I was just thinking of the post.' Edward spoke in gentle self-defence, then he observed that Dulcie was dressed as if she were about to leave the house. He knew what was required of him. 'I think you look very glamorous, Mrs Piper. *Très chic.*'

Dulcie's smile broadened. Then she led him into the living room and half turned one way and then reversed and turned the other. He had seen Rita Hayworth do much the same thing in *Cover Girl.*

'I'm glad you like it, Edward. Most people around here haven't got your knowledge and taste. I don't know who you take after in your family. I can't think of anyone on either side who you resemble. Still, nature is sometimes very kind. Orchids grow in swamps, you know.'

Edward admired Dulcie as she stood posing in her own living room, with her fingertips just touching the highly polished sideboard. She wore a red pill-box hat with eye-veil and a leg-o'-mutton sleeved coat and long, swinging skirt all in royal blue.

'I'm still the only person in this village wearing the New Look. Of course, you've got to be able to carry it off and, well, I shouldn't be wicked but can you imagine most of the women around here attempting to wear high fashion?'

'Not really, no.' Edward shook his head in resigned confirmation.

From the sideboard drawer, Dulcie fished out a pair of white, elbow-length, cotton gloves which she pulled on to either hand to complete the ensemble. With her puce face powder and cherry red lipsticked lips, Edward felt she looked patriotic; a kind of living Union Jack.

'Does your mother wear gloves?'

'Sometimes. Mostly on a Saturday night when she goes to the club with my dad.'

'Oh, dear dear. I couldn't go out not wearing gloves. I'd feel half-naked.' As if to remind herself that she was now indoors, Dulcie removed the gloves and placed them back inside the drawer. She let her fingers trail along the sideboard until one finger came to rest close to a cut glass vase filled with water and plastic flowers. 'Notice anything new?'

The profusion of blooms could hardly be missed. Not only were the colours garish and unsubtle but the false flowerings were entirely out of season as tulips and daffodils were well past their prime in June.

'They look lovely, Mrs Piper,' he lied. 'Very colourful.'

She beckoned him towards her, as if to share some great intimacy in a crowded room.

'Put your nose to them. Go on. Sniff them.'

Edward felt that Dulcie was experiencing some temporary derangement. Perhaps the new rig-out had turned her head. Nevertheless, he didn't wish to upset one of his best customers and did as he was bidden.

'What do you think of *that*?' Dulcie cried out triumphantly.

'I'm speechless.' How a bunch of plastic spring flowers could gain any authenticity by smelling of *Californian Poppy* perfume was well beyond his reasoning. 'Your sideboard's supporting a miracle, Mrs Piper.'

'Oh, Edward, you do say the nicest things. You have a lovely turn of phrase. Yes. It was all my own idea. I'm sending it off to the *Household Hints* in the paper. If it doesn't win a prize, there's no fairness in the world. Sit down and I'll get our tea ready.'

Part of Edward's visit to Dulcie was always taken up in this way. She would sometimes talk to him, calling out from the kitchen as she assembled a tray. Teapot, cups, saucers, small plates, milk jug, sugar bowl, paper serviettes were all carefully set out. Dulcie entered as though she were presenting a banquet but the fare was all ceremony and appearance rather than content.

'Ah, that's good.' Dulcie was self-complimentary as she sipped her tea through barely parted lips. Her tiny rosebud mouth always left a perfect pink lipstick imprint on the side of the cup. Tea which tasted like sweetened hot water and a single arrowroot biscuit each was fussed over as though it were a feast. It was very difficult for Edward to nibble on a single biscuit for twenty minutes in the same way that Dulcie did. He could have finished it off in seconds but bided by the rules of the house. Even in using his serviette to wipe off imaginary biscuit crumbs that might have settled on his lower lip. In spite of this, he enjoyed his time spent with her. Dulcie's unpopularity in the village, her snobbery, her poorly veiled dislike of his mother, all enthralled and fascinated him.

'I know I'm apart here, just as you are, Edward. We understand each other. I've never worked, you know. I helped my mother when she kept the wool shop but only until I was seventeen and then I married. I've always believed a woman's place was in the home. And what a home I've made for him, haven't I?'

Dulcie had made it known that her husband was *in business* in Wolverhampton. After a time it was revealed that he worked in a large furniture store which specialised in rotten hire purchase deals for gullible newlyweds. And some people even said that he worked in the warehouse and not on the sales floor. He was rarely seen as he never arrived home before seven pm and once there he either languished in the domestic comforts surrounding them or slept.

'Of course, I would have liked children. Not a houseful,' Dulcie shuddered at the thought, 'just two, or even one if they'd been like you, Edward. Is your mother going to let you learn to play a musical instrument?'

'I don't think so, Mrs Piper.'

'A pity.' She shook her head, visibly saddened. 'Not even the piano?'

'No. We don't have one. Do you play? Do you have a musical skill, Mrs Piper?'

'Well, I have the skills. They're within me, as they are within you. But who would bring them out here, in this area? Tell me that.'

'There are some places where you can go for piano lessons.'

'Oh no. Oh no, dear. I'm interested in classical music and piano players are ten a penny. If someone's singing, how often do they name the pianist? And they always look so dowdy, don't they? I could never be an accompanist.' She bent forward and fixed Edward with her pale brown, almost yellow eyes. 'It's the xylophone that my calling is for. You never hear anyone singing accompanied by a xylophone, do you?'

'Perhaps you could have lessons.'

'I dare say I'd pick it up quickly enough, but where could I find a suitable tutor. Not in these parts. And what's worse, if I became a successful concert artiste, people would give me hell around here. It's bad enough as it is. They're all so jealous if someone has a bit of class. Does your mother mind you being so . . . so . . . er . . . *different*?'

Edward did not want to commit himself to such blatant disloyalty and he was well aware that many people in the village considered Dulcie a dangerous woman. 'More tea, Edward?' Dulcie held the teapot poised in the air, its spout pointing at Edward as though it were some kind of lethal weapon. 'Well? Does she?'

He avoided the question.

'I don't think she thinks that I am different.'

Dulcie lowered the teapot.

'Oh but you are, you are. I only pray to God that she appreciates how she's been blessed, having you for a son.' Edward had bowed his head, wishing to appear modest in the face of such pious flattery. Dulcie bent forward and patted his hand. 'Never mind, dear. You know there is always someone here to talk to if you have any problems at home. All you need is understanding.'

Edward stood and nodded a smiling thank you and half-glanced at Dulcie's cuckoo clock indicating that it was time for him to leave.

She saw him to the door of the verandah and placed her hand gently on his shoulder in a form of hopeless restraint.

'Do remember – and this is strictly between us two – do remember there's always a pillow in this house where you can lay your head if you have a mind to, when you're working. It's your choice, you know.'

'Thank you, Mrs Piper.' Edward muttered as he moved slowly out of the orbit of her touching hand. It remained hanging there, limp in the air, as though it had been abandoned.

Today, Edward had brought forward Dulcie's visit by a couple of hours. He had a busy late afternoon ahead of him. The drama and elocution classes were to be followed by the costume fittings and in the evening he had agreed to help out at the Dog and Cat, alongside Costello's mother. And Costello himself, if he was in the mood. Last week he had not ventured into the bar but had remained in his living room, playing soppy songs on the piano.

'I think I should ask Roland to come and give us a

hand,' Edward had conveyed his thoughts to Costello's mother as he handed in empty glasses over the bar.

'Oh no, dear,' his mother had sounded alarmed. 'Not when he's in a decline.'

'Whatever's that?'

'I'm not sure, but only artists and poets get them.' She had smiled and added reassuringly. 'You and me won't have them, Eddie, so don't worry.'

As Edward walked briskly past Dulcie's grotesque statuary, he felt relieved that the time-span of his visit was to be shortened by circumstance. It was still true that he wanted to leave home just as soon as was possible, yet the idea of moving in with Dulcie Piper gave him deep forebodings. In fact, he'd rather stay where he was than do such a thing. The idea made him feel as if Dulcie were kidnapping him.

'I want to live alone and cook for myself and do my own washing and have a bath every day,' he thought.

The verandah door was slightly ajar and even before Edward stepped inside the glass lean-to, he heard the noise. He stepped forward then stood frozen to the spot. He held his breath, not in anticipation but in fear. A paralysis hitherto unknown to him seemed to envelop his body.

'Ow. Ow. Ow. Ah. Ah *OW!*' Screams and terrible sounds were coming from Dulcie's living room. If it were Dulcie who was making them then she was being attacked or robbed.

With a degree of courage that he found surprising, Edward moved a chair in front of the living room door and carefully placed himself in a standing position just beneath the windowpane above the door. One look, one stolen glance, was enough to cause him almost to fall backward in fear and trembling. Somehow he managed to get down from his viewing point without mishap. As in any nightmare connected with escape, his legs felt like leaden jelly and it seemed he could only move them with great effort. He had sufficient presence of mind to put the chair back in its original place before he left. Once in the street, he began to run towards the police station. He had a civic duty to uphold. How many people in the village or even in Batsford had ever witnessed a murder and reported it? He saw himself in court giving an eloquent account of what he had seen.

'Court? Court? Oh God, if I go to court, my Saturday job is finished. I'll have to leave school and they might even send me to a remand home for a few months.' With these thoughts invading his brain, he left the pavement and crossed the road and ran back towards his own home. His father would have to report the matter. He'd have to tell his dad about it. He couldn't expect anything but trouble from contact with the police.

'You're not going to put a tie on, surely?' Edward showed a considerable lack of filial respect as he addressed his father.

'Well, I don't get much chance to wear a tie during the week, do I. Your mam bought me this from Fosters. Top quality. It's top quality.'

Edward had delivered the dreadful news to his father and was shocked at the indifferent response it had received.

'Oh ah. I'll just finish this cup of tea then and I'll come down with you and look things over.'

He was surprised by this behaviour as it seemed entirely out of character and now his father was putting on his best tie as though he were going to one of his cousins' weddings or going to the working men's club.

'How's that, then?' His father turned for Edward's approval with regard to his neckwear.

'Dad! Don't you realise, Dulcie Piper is being attacked? Murdered! Don't you understand?' Edward's distress could no longer be contained. A residuum of panic was still all about him. His father sought to calm him.

'Well, our Edward. If she was being murdered, she'll be dead by now and there's nothing you or I can do to bring her back. The man was throttling her, you say?'

'From what I could see, yes. Come on. Come *on*!'

On the way to Dulcie's bungalow, his father stopped twice to exchange the time of day with people. He talked about pigeons, an unproductive coal seam at the pit, and some man who had not received any compensation for an accident sustained on the conveyor belt. His father had always been a neighbourly man. By now, Edward had definitely decided that there was a callous streak in his father's nature of which he had formerly been unaware. He felt the lack of concern for Dulcie's plight was shameful and he was about to put his indignation into words when his father caught his elbow and steadied his pace.

'No need to rush, Edward.' He nodded towards Dulcie's garden path. 'There's PC Higton leaving the house, so if anything untoward has happened, he'll do something about it. No need for you to report anything to anybody now, is there. You just go on about your business the way you normally would. I'll make me way back home as your Uncle Jack is coming round for me. We're going to have a game of bowls.'

He patted Edward on the shoulder and left. Edward crossed the road, intent on moving straight up to Dulcie's verandah door without pause, but now he stopped and thought of what he had seen half-an-hour ago. He could see himself standing on the chair. He could see himself looking through the pane of the fanlight. He could hear Dulcie's wailings. Now he could see the figure of a naked man lunged forward over Dulcie's best armchair. One of his huge fleshy buttocks – was it the left one? – was almost entirely covered by a red birthmark which was shaped like the map of Australia. Thank goodness he was good at geography. One of Dulcie's legs was splayed awkwardly over the side of the armchair whilst the man seemed to be holding the other one over his shoulder.

'Poor Dulcie. What a way to die!' Edward thought. No-one else in the village painted their toe-nails and Edward recognised the colour. He had seen the nail varnish bottle. *Pearl Pink*.

Five minutes later he stood outside the verandah and was puzzled to find it slightly ajar in the usual way. Surely PC Higton ought to have left a note on the door authorising that the whole house was under investigation and should not be entered? Hadn't he thought about fingerprinting and all those kinds of things? He stopped inside the verandah and put his ear close to the living-room door. He could hear a faint movement, as though curtains were being drawn, or was it the rustling of a dress? He tapped lightly on the woodwork with the knuckles of his fingers.

'Who is it? Who is it?'

Edward could scarcely believe his ears. He could never mistake Dulcie's trilling pitch. Not only was she still all in one piece, but she sounded in perfectly good health.

'You're early, Edward.' Dulcie's greeting lacked its usual pleasant effusion. By any standards, it was a tepid welcome. Edward gave his truthful reasons for the change of time and Dulcie's manner became less chilled. 'You say Councillor Elsie Phelps is playing Queen Elizabeth? Surely she can't act? She can't even speak properly. Is it a real horse she will be sitting on? Her hair is the wrong colour, anyway.'

'I think she's wearing a wig. The same as Queen Elizabeth did. She only says three lines. Just welcomes people to the pageant.'

Dulcie drew attention to her attire, a floral patterned quilted housecoat and some blue peep-toe slingback mules, which slotted on to her feet. 'Don't call before midday for the future, Edward.' She leaned forward. 'I know you will understand. Saturday morning is my quiet time, the time in all the week that I keep apart for reflection and reading. It's precious to me. You understand, don't you?'

'Perfectly, Mrs Piper.' Edward's gaze was drawn to Dulcie's foot. As she crossed one leg over the other and arranged the folds of the housecoat, one of her mules plopped onto the carpet. The toe-nails waved in the air. Five blobs of *Pink Pearl* flashed in the air before his eyes and he suddenly saw the sordid truth behind the tableau that had so chilled his blood. He felt himself blush hotly, but she chattered on, oblivious to his discomfort.

'I've been reading most of the morning. Time has flown by.' She waved her hand towards two paperbacks which rested on the floor beside her chair. 'I love the classics. I could read them over and over again. Georgette Heyer, Barbara Cartland, Angela Thirkell. They are what I call real writers. I have my prescription ready for you.'

'I wish she'd say *bet* when she means *bet*,' Edward thought. He felt an overwhelming dislike for Dulcie. He longed to be out of her living room as if by staying there for any length of time, he might contract some deadly virus which would pollute his mind. No longer did Dulcie amuse or fascinate him. What if he suddenly said,

'I saw PC Higton fucking you less than an hour ago. It was you who got Mr Starsbrook arrested. You are a quisling.' Instead, he took the ten-shilling note from her and smiled politely. As she escorted him to the verandah, he heard his own voice giving evidence in court above her vindictive prattle. 'Yes, my lord, I saw PC Higton doing his will, her will upon her.'

Dulcie's garden creatures, which always seemed fey, colourful and sweetly absurd, now looked somehow evil and malevolent and Edward quickly drew his attention from them as he passed by. Once free of her treacherous presence and overpowering environment, he felt imbued with new confidence and the first dawnings of adult insight. His job was secure now and when he left he would pass on the information to Mr Starsbrook who could not be betrayed by Dulcie or prosecuted by PC Higton. As for romance, what he and Lawrence had done together seemed a damned sight more appealing than what Dulcie had been up to. It was true, Lawrence hadn't kissed him first, but then boys didn't kiss boys. Or, if they did, he'd never seen any record of it anywhere, not in books, or on the wireless, or at the pictures. It was as though he didn't exist, nor Costello for that matter.

'If he's in a decline tonight, my news will snap him out of it.' Edward could hear Costello's responses.

'Oh how *terrible*. How *common*! What sort of noise was he making? In an armchair? He could have broken her back. And he's ugly, you say? A birthmark on his bum . . .' Then, sadly, 'Not as bad as a stain on your character. That's what we've got, Eddie. Stains on our characters.'

'Not stains, Costello, just different patterns. Come on. Your mother needs help in the bar.'

CHAPTER TEN

Edward, like his father, was always punctual. The drama class was now into its fifth minute and Edward was beginning to wonder whether being on time was such a virtue. For the past three weeks, Costello had arrived ten or fifteen minutes late, missing the opening session, with a series of unfortunate occurrences which had delayed his presence. Edward knew that Costello could lie so well he even convinced himself he was telling the truth.

'Your hands are not hands. Look at them. Stretch them out. Shake them. Let your wrists flap. Extend your arms. That's it. Now there are sparrows attached to your wrists. Let them escape. Make them. Let them flutter. Let them flutter and be free. Wave your arms this way and that. Set your sparrows free. Loosen your wrists.'

Belinda Spight had received a teaching diploma from the Central School of Speech and Drama. If she had not been a star pupil during her time in London, this was not reflected either in Trentfield or Batsford. As far as anyone under eighteen was concerned, she was the Queen of Arts. Now thirty and unmarried, she was liked and respected by male and female pupils alike. Good teachers were rare and enthusiastic ones sparkled like gold nuggets in a ton of coal.

Costello had reached his usual conclusions as far as Belinda's spinsterhood was concerned.

'She's Catholic. I expect she's fallen in love with a married man whose wife has left him and gone off with somebody else.'

'If that's true, she can marry him. He's free. So is she.'

'Not if you are Catholic. You have to stay married if your partner is alive. Don't you know anything about religion, Eddy? What church do your parents go to?'

'I don't think they're interested. They never mention such things.'

'Catholics believe in miracles. My mother's aunty married a man and had to become a Catholic because her husband was born one. She suffered terribly from arthritis and could only walk on sticks. Her husband took her to a special place in Ireland where miracles happen. It cost him a fortune, what with the fare and everything.'

'Can she walk without sticks now?' Costello's narrative had fired Edward's imagination.

'She can't walk at all.'

'What?'

'She managed to get up to the altar or raised dais or whatever it was. Her husband said she could only manage it by crawling like a crab. And then she touched this relic. I think it's some bones which belonged to a saint's foot. And then she fell. Backwards.'

'How terrible for her.'

'Oh no. No, Edward. It was a miracle. She can't walk at all now but she has never been so happy. Her husband pushes her everywhere in a wheelchair and she doesn't have a trace of pain.'

Edward thought this was a dubious miracle by any standards but he chose to say nothing as it clearly meant something to Costello. Anything theatrical always held some appeal for him. With a look of grave patronage Costello added, 'I'd become a Catholic myself but it's not possible for me as I want to have a lot of sexual congress without babies.'

'Without love?' Edward had enquired, for his own interest.

'You don't need love to make babies. I do wish Belinda Spight would do something about her clothes. It's chic to wear black all the time but it doesn't seem to work for her in that way. It's as though she's been in mourning for a long time and forgotten who it was that died.'

After the fourteen students had set their feet, hands, arms and heads quite free, they were grateful to take a seat on one of the chairs that skirted the perimeter walls of the classroom. Costello had said that Belinda only did this bit of exercise for her own purposes as during weekdays she taught some netball and physical education at girls' secondary modern school in Trentfield and if she didn't do some PE herself, her joints would stiffen.

Edward took stock of her as she walked into the central floor space. Today, as always, she wore black, but on Belinda it looked more homely than dramatic. She was a tall, wide-hipped woman, with strong-looking sturdy legs and thickish arms. The large, hooped earrings dangling from either ear and the small gold cross on a necklace that nestled just below the hollow of her neck, added some degree of stability to her ensemble, which looked as though it might disintegrate in any number of places. Her box pleated skirt swirled just below her knees from a front view, but the hemline had come adrift at the back. One of her high-heeled shoes was distinctly shorter than the other and badly needed attention from a cobbler. Her tight-fitting, long-sleeved, black sweater with the sweetheart neckline revealed one of her elbows as it had burst through the seam-work. Her untidy hair, her heavy breasts and warm, affectionate manner gave her an appeal that was blowsy, comforting and attractive to most people.

'I'll hear some of your individual pieces first. There are a few improvisation exercises I want to introduce to you afterwards and I'd remind those of you who have parts in the pageant to remain behind for . . .' Her attention was drawn towards the door as sometimes would-be trainee typists looking for the floor above them wandered in by mistake.

Costello stepped just inside the room, rested his back against the door and held the back of his right hand over his brow and half-closed. Everyone present focused their attention. He eventually let his hand flop from his brow and fall to his side.

'I'm sorry I'm late, Belinda.'

'Don't ask him what's wrong, just direct him to a seat. There's a big lie coming. Don't say *Sit down*, he's already holding the floor,' thought Edward. He had come to the severe conclusion that Costello's performances outside the drama class were often more convincing than they were in it. He urgently needed firm direction.

'Why, Costello. Whatever's wrong?' Belinda's beautiful voice oozed genuine concern and sympathy.

'It's my grandmother.'

'Is she not well?' Belinda had never heard Costello mention his grandmother before and showed immediate empathy. Edward had heard her mortality used for an excuse on at least three or four different occasions. To Edward's knowledge, the poor woman had been hit by a bus and died on a trolley in the casualty department of Stafford Hospital, collapsed and died of a heart attack when she heard her eldest son had left his wife *and* choked to death on a fish bone that had stuck in her windpipe. 'She's dead, I'm afraid.'

This last statement brought murmurs of sympathy from the newer girl members of the class. Edward sat, stony-faced and unmoved. How could Belinda be so gullible? This was the fourth week in a row. Was she going to let him make these entrances throughout the year?

'Darling, I'm so sorry,' Belinda commiserated with Costello as though she meant it and took him gently by the elbow and guided him towards the vacant seat next to Edward. 'You really shouldn't have come.'

'Oh, I couldn't let you down, Belinda. You know that.' Costello spoke in breathy tones as he had seen an Ava Gardner film the previous week.

'You're so brave to come. Sit next to Edward. I won't hear your piece this week. It wouldn't be fair as you are so upset.'

'But I'd rather you heard—'

Belinda pushed Costello gently into a sitting position. 'I won't hear of it, darling.' As she spoke, she looked over Costello's shoulder towards Edward. He was certain she winked. He glanced at Costello, who now sat next to him. He looked truly bereaved now. Costello surely hadn't expected this ploy and Edward had never known him accept defeat gallantly. For his part, Edward admired the subtlety of Belinda's class discipline. He turned to whisper something to Costello but was cut short immediately.

'Don't speak to me. Don't do your piece either. Say you've got a sore throat or I'll never speak to you again.' Costello hissed out this command from ventriloquist's lips.

By the time the class was ended, Costello looked grim rather than sad. Belinda had requested that those students who were taking part in the pageant should return in an hour and a half for costume fittings. As they descended the college's stone staircase, he declared he had no intention of returning as he had another appointment.

'Are you meeting your granny's ghost?' Edward attempted to lighten his mood.

'How dare you speak like that about my grandmother. I've decided not to speak to you for some time.'

Apart from referring to Costello's granny with less respect than was due to her, Edward had caused resentment by receiving fulsome praise from Belinda for his rendering of Spintho's speech from *Androcles and the Lion*. Costello had said he was not up to taking part in any improvisations.

'Whatever suits you best, Costello, dear,' was all Belinda Spight had said and then carried on with the lesson as though he were not there.

They made their way towards the War Memorial. Edward managed to unchill some of the frozen atmosphere by regurgitating Dulcie Piper's antics. By the time they had reached the bowling green, all Costello's reserve broke when Edward graphically explained what he saw through the window.

'Did you see his dick?' Costello gasped and then added, 'I shouldn't be talking to you.'

'No.'

'How could you miss it?'

'It was hidden from view. Inside Dulcie Piper.'

His speech now fully recovered, Costello raised his arm and pointed with his forefinger to the War Memorial steps.

'Look,' he said. 'She's arrived.'

Edward raised his arm in order to catch the attention of a rather plump girl wearing a tent-like yellow coat, a uniform design much favoured by ample or pregnant women. Costello grabbed his wrists and pulled it down sharply.

'Just a minute.' From his inside pocket he produced some sunglasses with emerald green frames. 'There. You can wave now, if you like.' The spectacles and quiff of hair falling on to his forehead reminded Edward of a parrot. What a parrot would be doing in Batsford on a day of dark, low clouds which had condemned the populace to perpetual twilight, Edward couldn't say. He was a bit concerned that Costello would be partially blind, but he supposed Costello would accept the limitation for the sake of Art.

'The frames match the colour of your eyes.' Edward sought to improve Costello's mood.

'My eyes aren't green,' Costello snapped.

'What colour are they, then?'

'Blue. They are duck egg blue.' Costello was an expert on information about himself and Edward didn't think it was an issue worth arguing about.

Both youths now waved in the girl's direction and she waved back to them. A few passers-by paused and watched this semaphore action, looking first one way and then the other. When Costello felt that he had attracted the maximum amount of public attention with this greeting, he rose and made his way towards the Belisha beacon, Edward at his side.

'If I took Costello's elbow as we crossed the road, people who don't know us would think he was blind,' Edward thought.

He didn't take his elbow. He and Costello had never touched and had never considered touching one another. Edward's fascination with Costello was companionate rather than physical. There were times, even, when he disliked him and found it hard to understand the basis of his own continuing admiration.

Vivien Barber greeted them as she always greeted them, with a light kiss placed on the side of their faces.

This affectionate but somewhat effusive greeting was always reserved for public places, and nothing could be more public than the steps of the War Memorial in Batsford on a Saturday afternoon. These displays of affection for both youths had granted Vivien more attention from her peers than she would have otherwise received. For some time, many girls wondered which of the two she would eventually choose and secretly puzzled over the hold she appeared to have over them.

From the open windows of the snooker hall situated above the Montague Burton tailor shop, three or four youths, billiard cues in hands, surveyed the affectionate display. They had never seen boys act like this with girls before and felt a mild arousal in their loins. If Vivien Barber would let boys kiss her in front of all and sundry in the middle of Batsford, what would she allow if she were up against the wall in the alleys behind the Danilo cinema or the Co-op Hall ballroom? She was a bit on the plump side, but a nice big pair of tits and a soft bum momentarily transcended the appeal of Wolverhampton Wanderers or Aston Villa. They did not admit this to one another, as the collective impulse overcame the individual. They returned to their snooker. For the time being, most of their activity was confined to groups, whilst their inmost thoughts were elsewhere.

By this time Costello, Edward and Vivien had linked arms as though they were part of a chorus line or in more sedate terms, dance terms, the Palace Glide. They walked around Batsford externally unaware of its buildings and human geography, yet their experienced eyes missed nothing of what went on. Costello had said that when his time came up for National Service, he would enter the espionage section. Vivien had chuckled and said,

'They'll shoot you on sight if you wear those glasses.'

Still suffering from the slight inflicted on him by Belinda Spight, Costello seemed to get fresh inspiration from the church's squat tower as they crossed the square. He glanced at Saint George's flag, which fluttered gently in the mild May breeze and imprisoned her for life.

'I think Belinda Spight will end up in a nunnery.'

'Nuns don't have boyfriends.' Edward was fond of Belinda and thought Costello was being far too drastic about her.

'Well, she can't marry a married man.'

Edward noted that Costello's previous supposition had now become a fact but did not interrupt his friend, who went on, 'Some Catholic girls never let a man touch them unless they are married to him and then it's their duty so they have to put up with it. My mother says they have to pray after they've practised sexual congress.'

'I can't believe they get out of bed half-way through the night. It would spoil everything.' Vivien spoke from imagined experience. Costello guessed as much.

'I think Belinda Spight is suffering from an internal struggle on account of the married man. That's why she wasn't up to the mark in our drama class today.'

'What man?' Vivien asked.

'I can't say, but he's not divorced even though his wife has gone off with somebody else. Catholics don't allow it. Poor Belinda. I suppose that's why she's so short-tempered. It must be terrible to be in love with somebody and not do anything about it.'

'They might do something.' Vivien was beginning to feel terribly sorry for Belinda.

'Very little.' Costello removed his glasses and shook his head. 'She might let him kiss her and touch her, but not above the knee or below the waist. As it is, she has to tell the priest everything.'

'What? *Everything*?' Vivien was deeply shocked and could not keep the concern from her voice. 'Poor woman.'

'Oh yes. Everything. And I mean, everything. Then he forgives her and tells her not to do it again.'

'You mean she has to tell the priest if she kisses him?' Costello nodded.

'She'll be a nun. I know it. I hope she's not condemned to silence. In some nunneries they are only allowed to speak on Christmas Day.'

As they moved towards the picture house, Edward was pleased with an opportunity that might allay any more punishment for Belinda – she had already been sent to a nunnery and now she had been struck dumb by God through Costello's mouth.

'Look. Look!' He nodded towards the road junction: Vivien and Costello beamed out their lighthouse gaze and absorbed the focal point of attention.

There was nothing new in seeing Angela Gayle and Olive Goodman together. Outside their working hours they were rarely seen apart. Now it seemed that their togetherness included their means of transport as both women sat confidently astride a brand new Raleigh tandem. There was a certain dashing appeal about their bottle-green slacks and lemon cable-stitch pullovers and an intensity about the way they craned their necks forward waiting for a pause in the flow of traffic.

Edward felt like cheering as the two women flew by them, heads held high, legs synchronised to perfection as the four feet pressed on the pedals.

'I think Olive should sit at the front,' Costello said.

'But Angela is taller. She has a better view of things. She couldn't see anything if she sat behind Olive's bum,' Edward defended his friend.

'If Olive puts on any more weight, the front wheel

will leave the ground and they'll have an accident.'
Costello tried to present this point of view as though he
were a technical engineer.

'I'm sure they take it in turns,' said Vivien, who was
eighteen months older than her friends. 'Sometimes
Olive's at the front and sometimes it's Angela. It must
be like that all of the time for both of them. They take
turns in everything.'

All three looked for signs of life in the milk bar. The
Wurlitzer jukebox was playing the Rex Ritter version
of *High Noon* and there were only two youths in
powder blue suits and black sharkskin shirts attempting
to look bored, drinking milkshakes and smoking as if
their lives depended on the strength of their inhalations.
Vivien sighed audibly and suggested they would all have
time for a cup of tea at home, which was less than five
minutes' walk from the centre of the town.

Both Vivien and Edward would have loved to go into
the milk bar but Costello had deemed it to be *common*
and therefore out of bounds to all of them. The number
of places in Batsford that had come under this embargo
had increased rapidly in the past few months. They
couldn't sit in the British Restaurant or the milk bar,
shop in Woolworth's, visit the park if a football match
was being played or go to see any film if John Wayne
was in it.

Neither Vivien nor Edward could explain the kind of
magical control Costello seemed to cast over them.
When he was not present, they were not averse to
discussing his shortcomings.

'I don't know what I see in him. Honestly, I don't. If
he kissed me, I mean kissed me properly on the lips, I
think I'd die.' Vivien had pointed to her lips which
were painted a reddish purple. 'He gave me this
lipstick. It's *Cyclamen*; the same colour as his mother

wears. I think he's in love with his mother.'

'Or himself,' Edward had joined in the critical appraisal. 'Most of what he says is ridiculous and he is so unfair. All his homework is copied off somebody else. He's even in trouble over his handwriting. You know, he doesn't put a dot over the letter i, he draws a circle around the top of it. If you look at a page of his writing, it looks as though there are bubbles floating all over it.'

And yet after these harsh scrutinies, they both always sadly agreed that he was the most exciting person to be with and their lives would be desolate without his company.

'I'm sorry, Vivien. I can't come back with you two. I've got an appointment in about ten minutes' time.' Costello half glanced at his watch as he spoke. 'I must be there.'

'I'll see you at the costume fitting later, then. Belinda says they are all ready with our names pinned on to them. There are over sixty of them hanging on the racks.'

'Where are you going? You never mentioned an appointment before now.' Vivien's sense of irritation had added boldness to her enquiry.

'A christening.' Costello lit a cigarette as Edward stifled a giggle. 'Could you give my apologies to Belinda Spight as I don't think I'll be back in time. Godparents have to fill in forms on behalf of the baby and make promises and that sort of thing.'

'But you're not old enough to be a godparent. And whose baby is it?' Even Vivien's adoration had been sorely tested by this latest excuse.

Edward knew that Costello's worst lies were always of a pious nature. Costello often quoted the Bible to prove a point and Edward knew that, as often as not, the quotation was nowhere to be found in the Holy

Book. Costello always said these things with such authority and conviction that it felt like blasphemy if you attempted to correct them.

He left them with a kiss on the forehead for Vivien and a reminder to Edward that he was expected to appear at his mother's pub at seven-thirty pm.

'He's a liar,' Vivien declared.

'We both know that. He seems to have forgotten he told Belinda Spight that his granny died this morning. He's getting birth and death mixed up. Perhaps it's his granny they're christening.'

Vivien took Edward's arm. The steady contact offered mutual solace for Costello's absence. His absence also offered an opportunity for them both to pay a flying visit to the library. Costello held all centres of learning in contempt. Vivien needed a Pitman's typing manual and Edward had promised to get a Zane Grey western for his father. As they left the library and skirted the car park, Vivien clutched so tightly on Edward's wrist that he almost called out in pain.

'Ssh. Ssh.' She propelled him behind the back of a large removal van. 'He's there. He's there! Costello's standing near the telephone box. He hasn't seen us.'

'We've a good view of him.' Edward nodded towards Costello's image which was clearly reflected in the wing mirror of the van.

They waited for what seemed like hours but was only a matter of minutes. They saw an RAF corporal walk past Costello and they noted the subtle kind of silent message that passed between them. The RAF man moved out of the mirror screen so that Vivien and Eddie were forced to move to the rear of the furniture van to watch his progress. He looked about him in the way that thieves did in second feature films, then, in a matter of yards, he opened the door of a black Morris Minor car and seated himself behind the wheel. He started the engine then pushed open the passenger door.

Costello came into view and it looked as though he were going to walk right past the open door. Vivien was about to call out, when Edward clapped a hand over her mouth. Costello slid inside the car and sat next to the driver. He slammed the door shut and sank down in his seat so that only the hair on the top of his head could be seen. The black Morris pulled out of the parking space, leaving Vivien and Edward staring speechless into a cloud of dust.

It wasn't hard for them to break Costello's embargo concerning the milk bar. They sat in the window seat and shared a large glass of Tizer, their straws placed on either side of the glass. Vivien stuck out her right leg and inspected her ankle and calf.

'I've laddered a stocking because of that bugger. He's the giddy limit. Of all the boys in Batsford, why do I have to dream about *him*?'

'I don't know.' Edward couldn't imagine how anyone could think of Costello in a romantic light. 'I don't dream about him.'

'I wonder who that man was?'

'Maybe it was Costello's older brother.' Edward didn't want Vivien to know too much.

'His brother is in the army and he's sixteen stone.' Vivien sucked hard on her straw, gulped down some liquid and then stared directly into Edward's face. 'I know about Costello, Eddie. I know about both of you. Don't ask me how I know, but I do. I won't ask you any questions and don't mention what I've said to Costello. I couldn't stand any more lies on top of what we've got.'

Edward shifted uncomfortably in his seat and somehow managed to break his straw. As his hand had begun to tremble, Vivien reached forward and patted his arm.

'Don't worry. You're safe with me.'

'Thanks, Viv. Can I borrow your straw?' Edward felt flooded with an overwhelming sense of relief. 'If I'm ever rich or famous, I'll buy you a car, I promise you I will.'

'I'll be happy with a new pair of stockings. You don't ever have to buy me anything, Eddie. I get a lot from knocking around with you – and that rat, Costello.'

'What? What do you get out of it?'

'Safety. I feel safe with you two. It works both ways, you know.' Such was the strength of Eddie's gratitude, he bought another glass of Tizer for Vivien and said he didn't want to share it.

CHAPTER ELEVEN

Edward waited for Belinda Spight's tinkling peals of laughter to subside. He had just given Costello's excuse for absence from the costume fittings procedure and this was her response. She didn't seem to be the slightest bit angry. Not even irritated. Eventually, after she had struggled to control a last chuckle, she said,

'Thank you for letting me know, Edward,' then giggled and added, 'What a Madam!'

A clothesline had been tied to either end of the room and several long black-out curtains had been pegged on to it, creating a serviceable screen which ran right down the centre of the room. Females were to change on one side of the curtain and males on the other. Belinda had suggested that those who wore simple costumes could help others whose apparel was a little more complicated. If there were any problems with regard to fitting or personal comfort then the matter should be brought to her attention.

'I'll pair with you, Edward, if you like. I might need some help with my rig-out. There are lots of bits and pieces to it and I'm not too sure where they all should go. I don't want to put things on the wrong way around.'

The male lead who played the handsome captain in love with Lavinia, prepared even to die for her, spoke beautifully without any affectation both off and on the stage. Costello had extracted, from various sources, all of his personal details. He was from Falmouth in Cornwall. He had lived in the area just over two years. He was seventeen. He was in some kind of legal apprenticeship at a solicitor's in Stafford. He lived with his older sister in a tiny house near the canal, a good six miles from Trentfield. His mother had died. His father had remarried, to a woman younger than himself. They still lived in Cornwall.

Edward raised his head as Bruce Tredennick was well over six foot tall.

'We had better find our costumes. They're hanging on the racks with our names pinned on to them.'

'I'll get them. You wait here. Keep this bit of space to ourselves,' Bruce volunteered.

Some of the twenty or so young men and youths were already in partial states of undress and Edward wrinkled his nose and wished urgently that some of them might discover the joys of apple blossom talcum powder by the time the dress rehearsal and final performance were enacted.

'There.' Bruce opened the window a few inches and laughed. 'That's better.'

Edward studied Bruce, who was busy looking for the right labels amongst the array of coat-hangers.

'He must be the scruffiest young man in the whole of Batsford. Not dirty. Not dirty at all. But he always looks as if he'd just woken up and put on the first clothes he could find.' He thought what others often said. Some even said it to Bruce's face but it hadn't seemed to make any difference. Today he was shirtless and wore a black, crew-neck pullover that had large holes in both elbows, a pair of baggy, grey flannel trousers, which were obviously some heirloom from a relative whose waist and bum were twice the size of Bruce's. On his feet were sensible black lace-up shoes, suitable for any office or a bank, but this trace of conservatism was ruined because Bruce had either forgotten, or chosen not to wear any socks.

At this point, Bruce turned and held two wire coat-hangers aloft, one a little higher than the other, and for one brief moment, Edward imagined him to be signalling as though he were a sailor on a passing ship. He was taller than anyone else in the room. Costello had said that he was gangly and clumsy and had no taste, yet Edward could see that Bruce didn't think much about what he looked like. What was more, he didn't give a damn how other people thought he looked. His hair stuck out all over the place and looked as though he'd never put a comb through it, and his face, like his body, was long and narrow, the mouth expressive, the grey eyes lively and full of humour.

'It's not going to take you long to change, Edward, is it?'

'Is that it? Aren't I going to wear anything else?'

Bruce handed Edward a coat-hanger on which hung a single, crimson satin garment.

'I think they called them togas. I'm sure you'll look good in it, Eddie.'

Still feeling disgruntled, in spite of Bruce's gentle condolences, Edward laid his costume carelessly on the window-ledge and began to undo his shoelaces as unhurriedly as possible. He had taken off one shoe when Bruce called out for his attention. Edward raised his head to see Bruce standing in just his underpants and vest. They were white and made of aertex cotton. He could see the dark hair through the tiny holes of the underwear and the shape of the genitalia, which hung down much further than his own.

'I'm not sure where this goes.'

'Around your waist. It's a kind of belt with thongs hanging down from it. A male skirt. There's probably a hook and eye at either end of it.' Edward felt annoyed with Bruce's ignorance and seeming helplessness. He really didn't deserve such a detailed costume if he didn't know how to put it on. And hadn't Bruce ever seen a Cecil B. DeMille film?

Edward took this opportunity swiftly to remove his own shirt, socks and trousers and then pull the crimson toga over his body.

'Can you give me a hand? I'm in a mess here, Eddie. I can't seem to find the – Oh. Oh . . .' Bruce stopped his artistic demands and looked at Edward as though he had never set eyes on him before. 'You look . . . I wish *you* were playing Lavinia. I'm sorry . . .'

Edward was not particularly concerned with what Bruce was saying. It was Bruce's gaze that intrigued and excited him. He had seen such looks directed at women by men, but not by a man to another man.

'He's lusting after me!' he thought and quite suddenly he experienced an odd feeling of control and power like he'd had that time in the pillar-box with Lawrence. He moved closer to Bruce, so that he stood directly at his side. 'Turn around,' he commanded. 'There. It's got a hook and eye. It keeps it in place around your waist. You look better as a Roman captain than you do in your usual clothes. Handsome in fact.'

'Here, Eddie. You've forgotten your wreath. These leaves, they're meant to encircle your head.' Bruce produced a comb and ran it through Edward's hair producing a small fringe of curls to lap his forehead. 'I reckon I could face the lions with more confidence if *you* were playing Lavinia. You look beautiful. You really do.'

'Kiss me, then,' Edward challenged this veiled lust or longing with a short whisper. 'Do it now.'

'I'm only joking, of course, Eddie. Only joking.' Bruce placed the wreath on Edward's head only for Edward to snatch it away from its mooring and cast it to the floor. Unable to control his rage and sense of injury, he gathered all his clothes together and marched away from Bruce without speaking or looking at him beyond casting a contemptuous glance at Bruce's hard-on. His skin burned with shame and he felt such a deep humiliation that if he had opened his pursed lips, a howl of anguish would have emerged from the back of his throat and sounded throughout Batsford. As it was, he quickly changed from his toga into his clothes, keeping his lips tightly closed and his eyes cast down towards the polished wooden floor.

Belinda Spight announced the dress rehearsal date and specifically asked Edward to pass the information on to Costello. Edward pretended to be in a terrible rush and barged his way through, past any number of players who were busy putting on or taking off their costumes. Only once did he glance behind him and then he saw Bruce in his aertex vest looking towards him. He smiled in Edward's direction and gently waved his hand.

Edward ignored both the smile and the faint gesture and turned quickly away. He hurried down the stone stairway, still feeling angry. Now his fury was directed at himself. How was it possible so suddenly to feel attracted to someone you had known for ages? And then, what was worse, how was it possible for you to be so plain nasty to them? Perhaps it was; even at this early point in life he felt that his rejection had been based on cowardice rather than lack of need or attraction.

CHAPTER TWELVE

For the past two years, an electric plug socket and kettle had been assembled in the back kitchen of Edward's home. This source of hot water was one of the few post-war luxuries that had managed to seep into the place. In the living room, the Elco radio set had been replaced by a radiogram and Edward's father now compared Mario Lanza with Gigli on 78 records. (Lanza's voice was louder but Gigli's sweeter.) As yet there was still no television set and the heating of the household was limited to coal fires.

'Don't use up more than one kettle. Every time you switch it on it's burning money,' his mother called out from the living room.

'Okay, Mam,' Edward lied. He was quite intent on using not one, but three kettles, full of hot water. How could she expect him to use the same warm water for his face that he'd used to wipe around his armpits, balls, cock and arsehole? It wasn't something he'd want to discuss with his mother. There were some boys of his age in the village who gave off a rank smell when you were sitting next to them.

Crack-hole, between legs, knob, balls, armpits – Edward gave them all a thorough wipe-over with a warm flannel before applying liberal sprinklings of apple blossom talcum powder to these areas which could be both enticing and revolting. After changing the water as quietly as possible he washed his face followed by either foot. Then, with a third kettleful, he washed his hair. He was only going to help out at the Dog and Cat but tonight some inner prompting made him want to have hair that shone like Lana Turner's.

'You through yet?' his mother called.

'Nearly done,' he shouted back, dabbing 4711 Cologne behind each ear with the bottle's stopper, the way he had seen Joan Crawford do. Midway through rubbing dabs of Nivea cream into either cheek he paused to look at his naked body in the cracked mirror, turning this way and that. He noted how hairs had grown under his armpits and around the top of his dick, springy and curly. Strangely, the hair on his head had begun to curl as if in sympathy. He had a horror of flattening this new feature down with Brylcreem or brilliantine like the other boys in the area. Instead he reached for a precious jar of Pantene, which Costello had recommended for its lack of greasiness.

He dressed again in hurry then opened the door to the living room and called through as airily as possible, 'I'm off then.'

His mother barely glanced up from her rug-work.

'The spare key will be on the ledge on top of the lavatory door. Don't wake us up when you come in and lock the back door after you go.'

She showed no trace of concern for what time he would be back, or even whether he'd come back at all. Striding off into the balmy summer evening, he wasn't sure whether to be peeved at this unmotherliness in her, or grateful.

Ann Costello was a huge woman. She was not merely big-boned or on the plump side; euphemisms like these did her no justice. She was huge. Not obese like Viola Settle, but built on a big scale, like a woman on a billboard. No-one had ever seen a Mr Costello. She kept no photographs of such a man or mementos of a marriage about the place. She made no references to him. If anyone was bold or foolish enough to drop enquiring hints, she would ask, 'Who wants to know?' in a voice of such awesome potency that everyone looked hastily into their glasses or at imaginary flies on the ceiling and the subject was speedily changed. Edward's mother, who praised nobody lightly, was fond of observing admiringly, 'That Ann Costello is man and wife in one.' Costello backed her up in this by boasting that his mother had brought him into being all on her own, by the power of her mighty will, and laid him as painlessly and purely as a chicken did an egg. Costello's knowledge of farmyard biology was as thin as his belief in miracles was unshakeable.

As a publican, she needed little assistance. She rolled barrels from brewer's dray to tap room with assured kicks from her stout-booted feet. Her huge hands made light work of wiping down tabletops and stacking chairs and her great arms were equally muscled from her crowd-drawing trick of pulling pints with each simultaneously. Some pubs might have a rough reputation but there was never any trouble at the Dog and Cat. In the early days of her stewardship, she had broken up a brawl by seizing two men by the hair, knocking their heads together then dragging them bodily out to the roadside by their belts. Word soon got around that Ann Costello was not a woman to be trifled with and that you could leave an infant or a virgin in her establishment even on pay day and see them come to no harm.

It was curious that such a woman should have raised such a boy. Edward might occasionally feel he did not quite belong but at least he knew he was human. Costello must look at his mother sometimes and feel like a creature from outer space. Certainly when the mood took him he liked to speak dismissively of her as 'a low creature' or 'a kind of *beast*' but Edward could see this was mere posing, for Costello and his mother used their lack of family likeness as the basis for a close friendship. They snapped at each other, as best friends might, but each took turns to play courtier to the other's queen. Ann Costello was a stranger to vanity but she allowed Costello to style her hair and choose her clothes. She would leaf through the film magazines to which they were both addicted and say, 'Go on, then. Make me look like her.'

'Ann Miller? Oh I hardly think so, Mother. So little dignity and her face is like a chipmunk's. No. This month I think you should be . . . Loretta Young!' And they would laugh at the challenge they had set themselves.

Watching them together, Edward had suffered moments of acute envy. Here was the mother he had always wanted; not a screen goddess – that he now saw was a childish fantasy – but a woman unafraid of cheerfully mimicking one. Unlike his own mother, who had little time for him much less for any friends he might have brought home, she made him entirely welcome from their first meeting. Stranger still, she not only knew about Costello's interest in men but, if Costello was to be believed, she indulged it.

The first time he invited Edward to a 'pyjama party' on the pretext of working on their lines, she assumed they would be sharing a bed. She laughed immoderately when her scandalised son put her right.

'Edward is like a *sister*, mother!' he gasped.

'Oh,' she had said, bosom shaking beneath her apron. 'I should have known. I'm so sorry, Edward.' She patted his small hand with one of her huge ones. 'I was going to say – I didn't think you were quite his type. I'll make you up a bed in the spare room, then you can *both* have company if you've a mind to.'

As she left the room, laughing to herself, Edward did not know where to look. His cheeks burned. He felt dizzy. These were things he had barely begun to say to himself and Ann Costello was saying them out loud, very out loud in her case, in her mercifully empty public bar. Costello saw Edward's discomfort and, in a rare moment of overt kindness, said, 'Don't mind her. Mother knows no restraint. She was thrown out of school by the nuns for *Acts of Lewdness*. She's a low creature but I can tell she likes you. If you don't want her matchmaking for you, just tell me and I'll soon put a stop to it. Otherwise she's like Mrs Bennett – wants to see us all well married.'

'But is it so obvious?' Edward stammered. 'That I'm . . . well . . . like *you*?'

Costello thought a moment, appraising him with narrowed eyes.

'Well, now that your dress sense is improving, it's beginning to show more than it did. But don't worry. Mother's simply more attuned than most, from living with me. She has a kind of radar for available men now. She sniffs them out at twenty paces. And she's rarely wrong, even about the married ones.'

Occasionally Ann – as she insisted Edward call her – was short-staffed and would call on Costello to swallow his pride and help her out.

'But I'd be obliged if you'd lend a hand too, Edward, since His Grace here insists on making every pint a work of art and his mental arithmetic's on the slow side too.'

She insisted on paying them the same wage as anyone else: 'So I can boss you around like my other girls,' but the money was only a part of the attraction of these evenings. Working behind the bar was like being on stage. The lighting was flattering, the bottles and glasses glittered about their heads like so many jewels, they were raised up slightly where everyone could see them and, best of all, they got to interact with men by the score, many of them new ones on visiting darts teams.

As Edward took orders, pulled pints, poured gins, added figures on the hop and remembered to return the change with a dazzling smile, he liked to pretend he was not really a barman but an actor playing a barman in a film. The only problem was that sometimes he was concentrating so hard on his neat little movements from bar to till to optic to bar that the figures went clean out of his head and he would have to apologise with a blush and take an order again.

Ann soon realised that she had to make them take it strictly in turns to round up the empties or she would find herself alone behind the bar all evening. Her usual staff hated the housework side of the job but Costello and Edward leaped on the chance to glide round the crowded rooms with a tin tray and a cloth, swooping on the not quite empty glasses of handsome men and neglecting to replace the full ashtrays at the less well favoured tables.

The evening was well advanced and the air was thick with smoke and beer fumes and Ann's rich contralto laughter as she bantered with regulars when Costello jabbed Edward in the ribs on his way to the till.

'Psst!' he hissed. 'Look what the cat just brought in. You'll have to serve him. *I'm* dealing with the darts team from the Hen and Chickens.'

Edward glanced up and saw Bruce Tredennick waiting at the bar. Bruce had dressed up for some reason. His white shirt wasn't ironed but it was clean, his hair was lying flat for once and he had on a dark blue moleskin jacket instead of his usual tatty overcoat. With his height and smooth skin, he stood out in the crowd like a prince at a workers' social. He was looking at Edward expectantly, eyebrows raised. Edward pointedly ignored him and served someone else. She was a woman he hardly knew and was bewildered at the rather aggressive show of friendliness with which he took her mundane order. When he turned to Bruce at last, it was with exaggerated politeness.

'Bruce. Hello. What a lovely surprise. Not your sort of place at all, I'd have thought.'

'Hello, Edward. I . . . I called round at your place.'

If Edward lost his cool, he did not let it show. He tried to sound smokily bored, like Lauren Bacall.

'Oh yes?'

'Your father said I'd find you here.'

'How right he was. Now if you don't mind, I've got people to serve.'

Edward was suddenly, painfully aware that he had acquired an audience. Not an imaginary crowd of cinema-goers but Ann Costello and the two women she had just served.

'I just wanted to say I was sorry.' Bruce's tone was beseeching. He might have been standing there stark naked, his desire was so exposed. 'About what happened . . . what I said at the costume fitting.'

'That's quite alright. Your usual, is it, Eunice?'

'Please lad, and a port and lemon for our Kath.'

To Edward's horror, Costello had returned from seeing to the needs of the visiting darts team and was pretending to polish a glass while blatantly listening in.

'The thing is . . . If you wanted to, that is . . . I was thinking we could—'

'Can I get you a drink, Bruce? Since you're standing there?'

'Oh. Er. Yes. I'll have a pint of best.'

'Right you are.'

Edward kept his eyes firmly on the glass as he filled it and took Bruce's money. As he handed back the change, their eyes met but he was determined not to honour the gangling fool with an answer. The sight of him, face flushed from his daring, eyes bright as a spaniel's, only reminded Edward of that afternoon's humiliation and hardened his resolve.

'Pass me the tray, Ann,' he said. 'I'll fetch some empties,' and he ducked out from under Bruce's gaze and Costello's scrutiny and lost himself in the jostling crowd. It took him five minutes to tour both rooms.

When he got back, Bruce had gone, leaving his pint untouched and Costello was protesting about something.

'I don't see why—' he began.

'I'd do the same for you,' his mother chipped in, raising a thick forefinger. 'You know I would. Now go and serve little Stevie Coles. He'll turn to stone if he stands there much longer.'

A momentary lull in demand had settled round the bar. She wiped up some spills with a cloth and watched Edward stacking empties beside the sink.

'I'll do those,' she said.

'It's alright, Mrs Costello. It gets my hands clean.'

'I said I'll do those, and it's Ann, as well you know. "Mrs Costello" makes me sound like a respectable widow-woman and everyone knows I'm proud to be neither.'

'But—'

'We're running short on lemonade. Take that crate out to the yard and bring in a fresh one. Here. You'll need the key to the bottle shed.'

It was a balmy night, not much cooler out than in,

but it was good to fill his lungs with fresher air. Edward
set down the crate of empty bottles on a stack outside
the back door. He leaned against the wall a moment
or two, staring up at the silhouette of a nearby tree
against a skyful of stars and enjoying the feel of the
brickwork on his hot back. When Bruce spoke, it made
him jump.

'Edward?'

'Good God! Where did you spring from?'

'The lady in there . . .'

'Costello's mam.'

'Is she? Yes, well, she said you'd be out here if I
waited.'

'I'll swing for her.'

'Edward please.'

'*What*? No. Listen. I've got to take more lemonade
in—'

He had been kissed before. Lawrence had always
fought shy of such tenderness during their field trips
together but Edward and Costello had successfully
persuaded several of the more manly boys at school to
part with money for brief 'kissing lessons' in the lavatory
cubicles. But he had never been kissed by someone who
meant it. Bruce took his head between his outstretched
hands and roughly drew their mouths together, forcing
Edward's lips to make way for a tongue he feared might
choke him and grinding his hips into Edward's so
passionately that Edward could feel the unambiguous
bulge of an erection pressing into his upper thigh. He
tried to break free but, as Bruce's hands slid down his
sweaty back and grasped his buttocks with surprising
strength, almost lifting him off the ground, his resolve
melted and he began to kiss back with equal abandon.
He thought of a passage Costello had secretly shown
him in a racy novel kept under his mother's mattress:

'*Feeling his powerful need for me, I lost all power to fight him off . . .*'

Bruce pulled back slightly to run his hands through Edward's hair and plant kisses on his nose and eyes.

'Oh Edward,' he sighed. 'I think I love you.'

'Don't be ridiculous.' Edward pushed him away, coming to his senses. 'You're only seventeen and you don't even know me. I've got that lemonade to fetch.'

He walked across the yard to the shed where the bottled drink was stored, trying to tidy hair and clothes as he went.

'Is that it?' Bruce pursued. 'I say I love you and you talk about lemonade?'

Edward turned the key in the lock then groped for the torch that hung on a nail just inside. He endeavoured to sound as cool as his mother might.

'Well, you can stay the night, I suppose. If you like.'

'What? Here?'

'Well I'd hardly take you home to my mam, now, would I?'

'But—'

'Ann's fine about it. She said I could. Costello has people all the time. You know. Men.'

'Kiss me.'

'Don't be silly. I'll drop the crate. Just lock the door behind me, would you, and put the key in my pocket. Just the key! You'd better stay in a corner out of sight until closing time or go and read a paper or something. Don't come in with me! People will talk.'

The bar had got busy again while Edward had been outside, so he was able to plunge back into work, stowing the fresh crate of bottles and immediately taking an order. Too late he caught sight of himself in the mirror behind them. His cheeks were as scarlet as his school blazer and his lips looked as though someone had been chewing them. Which, on reflection, they had.

'Everything alright, then, our Edward?' Ann asked when she passed him with four whiskies easily clasped in her hands.

'Yes, thanks,' he said, hating his voice for coming out as a squeak and unable to meet her eye.

'Spare room's all ready for you when we're through,' she said gently, and went about her business.

'Look at the state of you,' Costello exclaimed. 'Like a polecat on heat. You've been *cheap*, I can tell.'

'Button it,' his mother told him. 'Your turn'll come soon enough.'

Costello glared at her, slammed the till drawer shut and stalked off brandishing a tray like an offensive weapon.

'Oh Ann,' Edward said. 'I'm so sorry. From the way he talked about it I thought he was always, you know, having people back.'

'Oh no, Edward.' She looked almost shocked. 'That's just him showing off. You know how he gets. Another pint of mild, Stella? Coming up.' She frowned as she pulled the pint then sighed and he suspected she enjoyed the rare chance of bringing her precocious offspring down a peg or two. 'Sad really. None of his has ever been the bedroom sort, that I know of.'

Costello seemed in a less waspish mood when he returned from touring the tables. His mouth was no longer set in a tight little line. Edward assumed he had been flirting. In the corner near the fireplace there was a shushing as Beryl Allsop gave one of her clumsy flourishes on the ill-tuned piano.

'God help us. That Una Franklin's going to sing,' Ann muttered.

'My fault,' Costello said airily. 'I put in a little request.'

Mrs Franklin perched herself on a stool, leaned on the piano and sipped her stout.

'I've been asked to sing a little something for two shy lovebirds who are here tonight,' she said. 'When you're ready, Beryl.'

Beryl played a brief introduction then Mrs Franklin launched, with a coy smile around the gathered company, into *Love Is a Many Splendoured Thing* which went rather higher than her voice could comfortably compass.

The sex was nothing very special in itself. Bruce had been so traumatised by the waiting and the song – Una Franklin had sung all verses and had taken her time over them – that he had drunk more than was good for his self-control. It was all over in five minutes then he fell heavily asleep and snored. Edward was enchanted, however. He had been made love to in a proper bed with a brass bedstead in an attractive bedroom and now, like any married person, like his own mother in fact, he was spending an entire night entwined with someone who, before subsiding into snores, had repeated that they loved him. The sex was nothing special, but the sense of ordinary intimacy that followed was bewitching and he doubted he would ever settle for less again. As he drifted happily off to sleep, warmer than he ever was in his cramped bed at home, he made a resolution that from now on he was only going to take men of education and refinement as his lovers.

CHAPTER THIRTEEN

Bruce Tredennick woke in the early hours and dressed in a kind of panic. He muttered something about seeing Edward at the dress rehearsal, gave him a sour morning kiss and fled. There was no more talk of love. Edward did not greatly care. His mood of triumph was unassailable. If he loved anyone this morning, it was Ann Costello. Simply by giving her easy, no-nonsense consent, she had made him aware of possibilities. She had given him a real ambition to replace nebulous fantasies involving the likes of Montgomery Clift.

He was beginning to luxuriate in the novel sensation of sprawling in a double bed when the sound of church bells reminded him it was Sunday, one of his parents' Sundays away together. Resentfully he dressed and tried to tame hair which a brief taste of passion seemed to have turned to wire. He would have liked to do as he knew Costello would, and spend the morning in bed, but his conscience told him he should at least put in an appearance at home before his parents left in case there was anything they wanted doing about the place.

Apart from a brief spell of rank juvenile insincerity, when he discovered that books were given away as attendance rewards in the rival Sunday schools of the area, religion had played a mercifully small part in his upbringing. His parents saw to it that he knew right from wrong and attended school and left the rest up to the dictates of his heart. They were not churchgoers before he was born and, unlike some parents, did not acquire religion along with parental responsibility. His mother hated the sound of bell-ringing, deeming it an intrusion on her day of rest and was outraged when a pious acquaintance told her the bells were a weekly reminder that she was being prayed for. She saw no sense in allowing 'some man in a frock' to tell her how to behave when she knew already, thanks to common decency. Milder, his father said that what other people did with their Sundays was their affair.

'But there's the Church of England, the Methodists, the Baptists and my vegetable patch,' he said. 'And I know the first three can do very well without me.'

Sunday mornings had long filled Edward with queasily mixed feelings. He was proud not to be a churchgoer. His atheism, now that he had a name for it, was a secure rock of certainty from which to face the challenges of a troubling world. He disliked, however, the sense of being visibly marked out as a non-believer by being seen in the streets in his ordinary clothes by folk in their Sunday best. Try as he might to despise them for smugness or, in Costello's brave words, 'bourgeois hypocrisy', he saw their suits and hats, combed hair and scrubbed features and felt pitied and even diminished. The sensation as he walked past the gates of St Thomas's this morning, stepping into the road to make way for a clutch of little girls in straw hats and their harshly staring mother, was made worse by his growing belief that the people of Ardmoor had only to glance at him to know how and where he had spent the night. They could smell the sex on him and know that his cheeks had been rubbed pink by stubble not by virtuous soap and water.

The generous spell under which Ann Costello had

placed him had evaporated almost entirely when a familiar voice called out, 'Eddie!'

He turned and saw that he had just walked past Lawrence Brackenbury.

'Oh. Hello, Lawrence,' he said.

'Where were you off to so fast with your eyes on the ground?'

'Just home,' Edward said, hearing too late how strange this must sound at such an early hour. 'How are things?'

'Fine. Just fine.' Lawrence was got up in a new-looking jacket and waistcoat, his muscular neck straining in a collar and tie. 'Started work at Benmore's, then.'

'How's that turning out?'

'Not so bad. Fine, really.'

'Laurie?' A girl had come up. She wore cotton gloves and clutched a small black Bible. 'Come on, love. We'll be late.'

Lawrence took her arm in his.

'Sorry. Eddie, this is Katie. Katie Hines from Batsford. Katie, this is Eddie. Jack Warrington's boy.'

'Pleased to meet you,' she said and Eddie saw her eye his crumpled shirt and unruly hair. He saw her impatient squeeze on Lawrence's arm.

'We're to be married in August,' Lawrence said.

'Congratulations,' Eddie said.

Lawrence shifted his feet uneasily and Eddie wondered if he too was suddenly thinking of owls. 'Well. See you around, I expect. Say hello to your parents for me.'

'I will. Bye.'

Eddie stood for a minute to watch the young couple cross the churchyard and be swallowed up in the building's dark maw. Was this stiff creature really the same Lawrence, who had shown him where the best watercress grew and had offered him soft rabbits in his big fists like shy tokens of a courteous love? Labouring at Benmore's had already begun to work its noxious effects. His skin had begun to look dry. His eyes were pink and dim. Eddie imagined the girl, Katie Hines, kissing Lawrence. He imagined her sighing, 'Oh, Laurie!'

He tried and failed to imagine her naked but it was easy to picture her respectable refusal to let Lawrence go as far with her as he had with Eddie. He knew how excited this rebuttal would leave Lawrence, even if she was no Betty Grable. He tried to feel jealous of her power and was shocked to feel nothing beyond a thin kind of sadness, as at the death of a cousin he could scarcely remember liking.

He was dawdling up the lane, listening to the faint cacophony of rival hymn singing, lost in bleak thought, when he saw his parents up ahead, got up in their best clothes. His mother saw him simultaneously and waved him over.

'There he is! Come over here. Look at the state of you!'

'Sorry,' he began. 'I stayed over at the Dog and Cat because it got so late what with stacking the bottles and washing the empties and –'

'Well, I guessed that. Don't think we stayed up fretting, 'cause we didn't. But you made us late because Mr Starsbrook has been round and he needs to see you urgently.'

'We thought we should hold on to tell you,' his father added.

'I hope you haven't gone and lost your job. There's the bus. We must hurry.' His mother pulled his father along with her. 'We'll be back for tea as usual. You go home and clean yourself up before going to Mr Starsbrook. Show some respect.'

Mr Starsbrook was not at home when Edward called round at his bungalow. Bridget Casey was in the garden, though, tending the roses and she reached into her apron for a small pad of paper and wrote on it, *He's at Viola Settle's. You're to go there.*

She looked grave, not her usual smiling self, and as Edward hurried to Viola Settle's house he worried. Had he somehow taken a bet down wrong? Was he to be accused of robbery or fraudulence? Perhaps he would have money docked off his wages or, worse still, be sacked and sent back to the shame of riding a delivery cart? By the time he entered her narrow street, he had convinced himself that matters were even worse, that Dulcie Piper had shopped them all to the authorities, Mr Starsbrook was to be arrested and Edward, as his accomplice in a life of crime, was to be sent to some horrendous reformatory. Edward had watched a double bill of films set in prison, all hatchet-faced wardresses and sadistic lifers; he knew it was not an environment in which he would survive for long.

Mr Starsbrook must have been watching for him because he darted out before Edward could knock at the door and led him swiftly into the hall. His face was as grave as his housekeeper's and Edward's heart sank still further as he heard women weeping behind a closed door.

'It's bad news, I'm afraid, Edward.'

'Is it the police?'

'No, lad. It's Mrs Settle, one of our most valued clients as you know.' He put a hand on Edward's shoulder to reassure him. 'She died in the early hours of this morning.'

As if on cue, the sound of weeping from behind the closed door redoubled.

'But—' Edward began, wondering what on earth this had to do with him.

'As you probably know, her daughter had been trying to persuade her for some time to take a trip with the family to a holiday camp beside the sea. Well—' Mr Starsbrook dropped his voice to a respectful whisper so that it sounded less as if he were merely gossiping. 'It seems that Mrs Settle finally agreed to go and they were all packed and set to be off this morning but the excitement and the shock of the early morning start, with her daughter's electric alarm clock and everything, was too much for her. It was her heart. It just gave out. Very little suffering. A merciful end really and the holiday camp will be refunding her share of the deposit—'

'But—'

Before Edward could ask how this lamentable state of affairs concerned him, the closed door swung slowly open and Viola Settle's body was revealed, laid out in readiness for the undertakers. The weeping had stopped and her tearful daughter and granddaughter stepped out into the hall. To Edward's astonishment, the daughter drew him to her and kissed his cheek.

'Bless you for coming, Edward,' she said. 'I expect you'd like to go in and say goodbye.'

Like a sleepwalker, inexorably drawn, Edward walked in. The window had been opened to air the room and a light breeze made the net curtains dance. Viola Settle's hair had been brushed out about her face so that it shone and it, too, shifted in the draught. There was a touch of rouge on her rough lips, so that she appeared to be blowing a kiss, and where her hands were arranged to meet on the mountain of her belly, a small bunch of flowers had been tucked. A candle burned on the bedside table beside a faded photograph of what might conceivably have been Viola Settle as a chubby little girl. Its light caught the charm bracelet she still wore, and her battered wedding ring.

Thinking to back away, Edward realised the daughter was now close behind him. She nodded her reassurance when he glanced round, indicating that he should go forward. Awestruck, for this was the first body he had been allowed to see, though strangely unafraid, he found himself stepping forward and lightly touching his hand on one of Mrs Settle's. He tried to say, 'Goodbye,' but no sound came beyond a hoarse whisper and, hearing this, he was astonished to realise he might be about to cry. Gulping, in need of open air suddenly, he backed off into the corridor, leaving the women of the family together, and followed Mr Starsbrook out to the kitchen where he was given a biscuit and a cup of sweet tea.

'It was such a shock,' he said when he felt able, grateful for Mr Starsbrook's having waited for him to speak first. 'I know she wasn't the most active person but—'

'You've another shock to come, Edward,' Mr Starsbrook told him. 'Mrs Nesbitt, that's Mrs Settle's married daughter, the lady in there, says she wants you to have some token of thanks. She said you didn't just take the bets and move on but you used to spend time sitting with her mother and talking and changing her bandages.'

'I was only doing what you told me to, Mr Starsbrook. You said I should foster a relationship of trust with the client.'

'Quite so, quite so. But the family were deeply grateful and Mrs Nesbitt says you're to have whatever her winnings were from the last week's bet. And Edward, you'll never guess, but you know how she always betted on the names she liked.'

'Oh yes. Mrs Settle wasn't interested in form at all. I did try to explain to her but the names were all she seemed to focus on.'

'Well, it paid off. That outsider she backed yesterday—'

'Danny Boy.'

'He came in first! You're not rich yet, but you'll not have to raid your piggy bank for a few months.'

It was hard not to splutter his tea. The sum named was more than Edward could imagine counted out before him, maybe not even in the till at the Dog and Cat at the end of an evening. When his employer took a brown envelope from his breast pocket and slipped it across the kitchen table towards him, he was confused for a moment. Had Viola Settle had time to write him a note from her deathbed? It was with a shock of embarrassment that he realised he was being paid in discreet paper money, not in bulging bags of coin.

Walking home, he kept the envelope grasped firmly in his pocket. It felt so light and worthless. It was only once he was safe in his mother's kitchen that he dared open it and count his blessings. He hid it in the back of the box where he kept Farley Grainger, slid the box back under his bed then lay down and began to feel as guilty as a thief.

It was illegal money. Money badly come by. Worse than any fear of the police, however, was the nagging of his conscience as he thought of the hours he had spent in Viola Settle's company. He had been false with her, outwardly charming even as he was secretly disgusted by her size, her ulcers, her immobility. And she had taken it as devotion and rewarded him as a mother might a son. He thought of her great corpse laid out in state, he thought of her grieving daughter and grandchild and, inevitably perhaps, he imagined his own mother's death and how he would react to it.

He had pictured her death countless times before, of course. Whenever she crossed or slighted him – which at one stage had been several times a day – he had taken refuge in imagining her funeral. He planned what he would wear, how the coffin would look, how he would bravely hold back his tears while supporting his father in his deeper grief. Sometimes, when this proved less than satisfactory, he reversed the fantasy and pictured his own funeral, based around morbid photographs he had seen of Hollywood ones. He saw his open coffin, masses of white lilies and, best of all, his mother half-mad with the tragedy of it all.

Now that he had seen a real corpse, however, a real dead mother, his old fantasies seemed like broken toys. Rather than picturing her safely tidied into a coffin, he could now see her sick and suffering. If someone as reassuringly solid as Viola Settle could die merely from the shock of a puny alarm clock, how little it might take to finish off his mother. She was thin. She had always been thin. As a child he had never thought of hugging her or sitting on her lap, not just because she discouraged such behaviour but because, he realised now, she was the wrong shape. And now that he thought about it, he could remember hearing one of her friends commenting only the other day, 'Look at you, Esther. All skin and bone. You're wasting away.' The friend's companion had frowned suddenly as if warning her on to a different subject. Edward had seen this and assumed she was merely being polite.

He jumped off his bed and ran to his parents' room. In the next hours he made up for a lifetime of obedient Sundays. Not prying had always been the one rule of hers he chose to respect, perhaps from an unconscious trust that if he did not pry into her affairs, she would not pry into his. Now Edward did not merely pry, he went over her things as methodically as any secret agent. He opened every drawer, turned every key, scrutinised every scrap of paper he could find, taking care to leave everything precisely as he found it. Not that he cared, now, if she knew he had been prying. He had all day. He was determined to find proof and having found it, he would hold it up and confront her.

She was sick. Of course she was. Dreadfully sick. She had been sick most of his life, probably from cancer that was steadily eating away at her. He had always been faintly envious of her Sunday excursions with his father, assuming them to be pleasurable jaunts. Now he saw that they were trips to the hospital for treatment, treatment that left her sickened and exhausted, which was why she tended to be so quiet on her return. They had begun by not telling him in order to protect him from the truth and to spare her from his childish questions. But the sickness and its treatment had gone on far longer than they had imagined and now the secrecy had become a fixed habit, like filling the kettle or washing one's hands. Picking over old letters, postcards and handbills, he thought of how much the treatment and the travelling to and from hospital must have cost over the years and recalled, with a pang, all the times he had moaned about how little money they had compared to his friends.

He was not entirely sure what he was searching for. An appointment card perhaps. A bottle of bitter medicine he had not seen before, with her name on the label. An official letter confirming that she was sick. Very very sick. Dying even. A photograph was going to tell him nothing and he only glanced at the few snapshots he found out of idle curiosity. One, however, halted him in his tracks. He had been going through the drawer in which she kept her cardigans and pullovers and found it tucked between two soft layers. He sensed at once it had not been dropped there by accident but had been placed there. She had chosen this drawer because it was the softest and the most protective hiding space she could think of.

It was only part of a photograph, a narrow strip trimmed off a larger picture. It showed a little girl, no more than two. She was standing unsteadily, clutching a man's hand that reached in from the cut side of the image. It was an old picture, crumpled with handling and probably not of a high standard to begin with. The girl's face was not properly visible because she had looked down at her feet at the crucial moment and her dark hair had flopped forward, masking her.

Photography was not a hobby his father could afford so Edward knew the few significant photographs in the house as well as his own face. He had pored over them repeatedly as a boy as important proofs of who he was. They stood on the downstairs mantelpiece in old tin frames. One showed his parents, unfeasibly young in the week of their wedding. Another showed them a few years later clutching a bundle of shawls his mother had sharply assured him was him as a baby although there was no way of telling. The picture had always sat oddly in the frame, as though it had slipped to one side. Mother and baby were firmly on show but Edward's father appeared to be stepping out of the frame.

Feverishly Edward opened the back of the frame, bruising a fingernail as he prised away the little tacks which held the piece of wood in place. The picture and the scrap from the jersey drawer were not a perfect fit since the scrap was bent and roughened where the picture had been kept flat by glass. They belonged together, though. He could see that straightaway. His father was not stepping out of the frame but stooping slightly to hold the little girl by the hand. Edward stared, sucking his bruised nail.

He placed the picture back in its frame and sealed up the back again. He did not replace the little girl in his mother's drawer, however. He kept her on the table so that when his parents sat down to tea on their return, they should know at once that their secret was out. He laid the table hours in advance, brought in coal, then forced himself to sit quietly in a chair to read his library copy of *Cranford* to calm his nerves while he waited.

By the time he heard their low voices outside the door, however, he had worked himself into a fever of curiosity. He had planned a theatrical revelation scene but instead found himself presenting his startled parents with a garbled confession even before they had sat down.

'Mrs Settle died in the night and I saw the body, I had to, and that led me to thinking that what if you were to die, I mean, what if you were ill and that was where you always had to go on Sundays, for treatment, and I know I shouldn't but I started looking through your things because I had to find out in case it was true and I found that.' He pointed at the scrap of photograph beside the teapot, adding softly. 'Her, I mean.'

'Oh Christ,' his mother said softly and sat so suddenly and heavily that for a moment he thought she really was ill. His father only stood, still clutching his cap which he had been about to hang up. Faced with their solemnity and weariness, Edward felt very much like a child again yet strangely like an adult confronting two children over a misdemeanour.

'She died,' he said. 'Didn't she? When I was a baby. And once a month you go to visit her grave.'

His mother's voice was harsh.

'The graveyard's only down the road. If she was dead, we'd hardly be gone all day.'

'Esther—' his father began and laid a hand on her

shoulder. She shrugged it off impatiently, leaving him frozen.

'I've told you not to pry, haven't I? A thousand times I've told you. No good comes of it. The things you're meant to learn you'll be told.'

'I had to know. I thought you were sick.'

'Well, you had a bloody funny way of showing it.' She glanced up at his father. 'Stop hovering. Sit down and drink your tea.'

His father sat. His mother poured them all tea. The teaspoon's tapping as she stirred sugar into her cup made Edward want to break something. At last he spoke again, unable to bear the silent tension.

'So I've got a sister?' he asked uncertainly.

His mother nodded. She sipped her tea. For once in her life, she was not meeting his eye.

'So where is she? What's her name?'

'Lily. She's called Lily. She's two years older than you and she's not right in the head. Once you were born she was more than I could cope with so we put her in a home. She can't look after herself. Never will. So now you know. Satisfied?'

She left the piece of cake she had been nervously crumbling on her plate and hurried from the room. Edward's mother shouted and argued and fought her corner. She never did this. He had never seen her like this. He listened, amazed, at the sound of her hurrying up the stairs and shutting the bedroom door behind her. There was a faint creaking in the ceiling and he knew she had climbed on to her bed. He turned to his father.

'Why did you never tell me?' he asked.

'You never asked, son.'

'I was never allowed to. She told me to mind my own business so I gave up asking. I'd have wanted to know. I'd have wanted to see her. She's my *sister*.'

His father sighed.

'Your mam wasn't really telling the truth,' he said. 'She's painting herself black to save face. You know how she is. She loved Lily. In spite of everything. But the moment she knew you were going to be, you know, alright, she insisted. Lily had to go into the home, she said, and you were never to know anything about her.'

'But why?'

'She wanted you to be happy. She didn't want a shadow on your childhood. And Lily's alright. It's a good place. They're good people. We go to see her. We sit with her or push her around the garden in her chair. She doesn't really know who we are anymore but we still go. She loves you, you know. Your mother loves you. If she found it hard to show it was only Lily getting in the way. She'd think of Lily, feel bad and end up taking it out on you sometimes. Of course, when you turned out such a smart alec, it didn't help much either.'

His father smiled to show he meant this gently.

'What should I do?' Edward asked, utterly at a loss.

'Take her up a fresh cup. She's worn out.'

There was no response when Edward tapped on the bedroom door, but he let himself in anyway. If his mother had been crying, she gave no sign of it. He set her tea on the bedside table and beside it, the photograph of his sister which he had brought back upstairs as an afterthought. She murmured her thanks and moved her legs to make room for him at the bed's end.

'I suppose you'll be wanting to see her now,' she said. 'She won't know who you are, you know.'

'I know. Dad's told me. Would you rather I didn't?'

'You can do as you please. You usually do.'

Her familiarly abrasive tone was a relief. Edward had feared a tearful scene with her, still worse, a loving one, more than the wrath of God. He preferred her like this, whatever he might have just learned. It was what he was used to.

'Your hair looks nice.'

'Don't get round me that way. You were prying. You know you were.'

'I know. I'm sorry. But—'

'But what?'

'But I'm not sorry I found out.'

'No,' she said wearily. 'I suppose you had to in the end.'

As she drank her tea, he told her about Viola Settle's corpse and his unexpected windfall.

'I thought I could buy a nice dress.'

'You what?'

'For *you*, and a new cap for dad and maybe something for Lily.'

She shook her head.

'You save your money. She'd only break whatever you gave her. And anyway, Viola Settle meant that money for you, not us. It was you that used to bandage those filthy legs of hers. You earned it. Spend it wisely, mind. If you had any sense at all, which I doubt, you'd go into Batsford and visit Northcott's and get yourself a decent suit made. For that money you could afford it. Nothing fancy. Just plain grey flannel. But a well-made suit would last you a while, at least and the way you're going you'll not be sticking around here for long and you'll be needing smarter clothes.'

'But—'

'Just think about it, that's all. Don't do anything in a rush the way you usually do. Is the money somewhere safe?'

Reassured, she asked to be left in peace for a while and sent him downstairs to dig some potatoes to go with the pork chops they were to eat. Working with the fork in his father's vegetable plot, watching the pale waxy tubers emerge from the broken soil, Edward wondered at the alterations the last two days had brought. He was reminded of his bitter disappointment in fireworks as a boy, remembering how their displays had never lived up to the anticipation fed by their gaudy labels. Two days ago he would have said that the pageant was the most important thing in his young life. This morning he would have named, instead, his having passed the night in the arms of a man. Now he knew it to be neither of those things. He felt he had passed from a brightly coloured chamber into which there was no readmission. His mother was right. He would take the money into Batsford at the first opportunity and have a suit made. The boy in scarlet would have to give way to the man in grey, but he fancied his sober new jacket might sport a scarlet lining.

AFTERWORD by Patrick Gale

Discovering an unpublished novel in a dead writer's desk is a little like finding the scarred clay of the new grave transformed by freshly sprouted fritillaries. There was just such a discovery in the aftermath of Tom's death; a clutch of navy blue exercise books, their pages closely covered with his familiar scrawl produced with the stubby biros he liked to borrow from the betting shop.

There were in fact two novels. One he had been teasing me about for months because the title contained his camp name for me. 'I'm calling it *Angela's Men*, darling. You can look on it as a payback for all those weeks you were moping in my spare room and making me take all those fucking phone calls.' This promised, mischievous tribute to Mrs Gaskell had run to little more than half a chapter before his first heart attack and subsequent illness brought a halt to his writing altogether. There was, however, the work you have just read.

Tom had so many well-polished tales of his adolescence and seemingly charmed sexual initiation that several of us had long been asking him to write a sequel to his boyhood memoir, *Forties Child. The Scarlet Boy* is as near as he came to answering our hunger. His parents are in there, as are his cherished 'sister' Colin Dando and his mother Ann, thinly disguised as the Costellos, and his gleefully egotistical teenage self. It was as though there were other, painful elements caught up in the true story, however – the illness and death of his mother, his difficult relationship with his brother, Colin's tragically early death by drowning – which he found he could not confront. What he gave us instead was a tapestry of the familiar anecdotes and a fictional celebration of those elements of his teenage self that fed directly into his adult persona – his love of performance, his honouring of born educators (not necessarily school-teachers), his delight in literature, his worship of his father and his hatred of hypocrisy.

My problem was that this novel, too, was incomplete. It petered out at the point where Edward is preening himself for his night at the Dog and Cat. As it stood, it was unpublishable, peppered with the inconsistencies one would expect in a first draft. To 'complete' it seemed a monstrous breach of writerly etiquette, yet what I had read was so enchanting that to leave it unpublished would have been an act of cruelty to his readers and to him. There were a few pages of notes but the work's conclusion lay entirely in my hands. Tom never left loose threads in his plot so I had to assume that there was some significance in the parents' repeated mysterious absences that would be revealed. I thought of changing the days when these happened to a Saturday and linking them to some grim medical treatment the mother was receiving. Then it struck me that precisely his unwilling-ness to deal with this might explain why he dropped off from writing where he did. Instead, as a way of honour-ing his educative achievements in the various special schools he transformed, as well as respecting his qualms, I came up with the surprise sister solution. When it came to the nearest Tom allows us to a romance, I confess I indulged my own romantic tendencies in at least allow-ing Eddie one night of albeit clumsy passion with Bruce

Tredinnick. I wrote it drawing on what Tom had told me of Ann Dando's generosity and felt I could balance any sugary effects against Tom's more citric outlook as reflected in the events of the morning after.

There were numerous small changes to be made throughout, notably in Tom's revealing habit of letting the 'real' names pop up in place of the fictional ones, but I nobly resisted the temptation to edit out his casting of my lover and myself as an ambulance driver and her librarian girlfriend . . .

Writing in another writer's style is never easy, particularly when they are a friend. All I could do was stifle my love of subclauses and remember that Tom wrote the way he spoke. It was better that the novel should be published as some hybrid of our styles, a testament to friendship in effect, than not at all. I hope that his loyal readers will agree, and forgive my trespassing into cherished territory.

Cornwall, October 1997

Also by Tom Wakefield
and published by Serpent's Tail

Forties' Child

An Early Autobiography

It is the 1940s. The world is at war. Here is the period
viewed by a small child growing up in the very heart of
England. Through his eyes, we see how the conflict affects
a working family, how external events shape the domestic
clutter of daily life. We are presented with vignettes –
drawn with a childhood sense of wonder – of both high
comedy and tragedy that reflects his increasing awareness.
Void of sentimentality *Forties' Child* is not lacking in
sentiment. In its unique, autobiographical way, it indicates
how – given that the wounds of war are not received solely
on the battlefield – ordinary people can triumph over
extreme adversity.

'This is a tender and original recollection of the way a
child puts the amazing world together, by a writer with a
gift for leaving raw things raw.' *Guardian*

'I greatly enjoyed Tom Wakefield's classic autobiographical
account of a wartime Midlands boyhood.' *The Times*

'What disarmingly polished scenes they are . . . Tom
Wakefield is one of our most engaging of novelists.' *TLS*

'Through his detailed, accurate and incisive observances
and remembrances there exudes a natural unforced
sentiment which prove both genuinely heartwarming and
eminently readable . . . It's one of those books that cannot
be put down, and once finished demands to be read again.'
Time Out

'Beautifully evoked, touching and immensely readable.'
Gay Times

Lot's Wife

Henry Checket and Peggy Thurston have been forgotten by society. They spend their final years in an old people's home run by the domineering Veronica Fairhurst. Each brings with them a past life, of pleasures and regrets, that they neither want nor are able to forget. As their relationship develops, they each discover much about their true selves, including a shared inclination to rebellion. Steering a fine course between comedy and tragedy, *Lot's Wife* proceeds with verve and passion towards the unexpected dramas of its conclusion. Tom Wakefield's new novel will delight his readers, old acquaintances and newcomers alike. It is the work of a most gifted writer who, rare for today, loves and empathizes with his characters.

'[Tom Wakefield's] past work has always been so consistently excellent, you wonder if he could produce something better. Well, he has. Breathe a huge sigh of relief and settle down to enjoy his latest honest, deep and winning book which will not only delight the author's multitudinous fans, but will also gain him many new admirers.' *Time Out*

'Comic, scathing and oddly gentle fable about love and subversion in an old-people's home in England.' *Los Angeles Times*

'Wakefield's empathy with his characters, with the plight of the outsider and the importance of personal dignity, has created a sensitive and moving book.' *Sunday Times*

'This is a very funny, very moving and acutely perceptive book, which I highly recommend.' *New Statesman*

'A mordantly touching tale of platonic love and rebellion set in a nightmarish retirement home.' *Daily Telegraph*

The Variety Artistes

An elderly widow, Lydia Poulton looks set to end her days in the loveless embrace of her family where roses receive more nurturing than people. A chance meeting at the local 'Know Your City' class brings Lydia face to face with the realization that whatever others may think she is still very far from ready to 'settle down'. Whirlwind romance, the friendship of another woman and the lure of the foreign infuse Lydia's life with overwhelming passion. Once again, Tom Wakefield has magically given an ordinary life an extraordinary dimension. With the empathy and compassion that are the hallmarks of his skill as a writer, he enriches our understanding of what it is to be old, alive and kicking.

'Wakefield possesses a keen sense of drama and draws some wonderful, almost theatrical "scenes" which can be re-read, enjoyed and savoured, and his characters are full-bodied, living creations who quickly become familiar and memorable. Warm, sensitive and witty.'
Time Out

'A lovely story . . . a gentle, humorous parable that says: Watch out – given the chance, there could be a lot more to that compliant old woman than meets the eye.' *New Society*

'Full of humour, tenderness, humanity and confidence in life.' *Gay Scotland*

'Somewhat picaresque, intensely human, richly comic, *The Variety Artistes* is an absorbing and ultimately deeply moving novel.' *Gay Times*